To Brendan —

Sincerely yours,

Julian Bagley

Candle-Lighting Time in Bodidalee

By Julian Bagley

Illustrated by Wallace Tripp

With a Foreword by Dr. Alfred V. Frankenstein

AMERICAN HERITAGE PRESS, NEW YORK

To Remember John Lund Mikelson

Contents

Foreword

Julian Bagley is a connoisseur of opera houses and of the black man's folk tales. This may seem an unlikely combination, but it is a thoroughly authentic one because Julian Bagley is a thoroughly authentic personality. He appears, of course, between the covers of this book in the second of the two connoisseurships just mentioned. In the first, he is celebrated throughout the entire musical world, especially on the Pacific Coast.

Mr. Bagley has not missed a single performance at the War Memorial Opera House in San Francisco since it was opened in the fall of 1932. His official title there, although it is little known and fits badly with the West Coast milieu, is concierge; his principal activity is conducting tours. People come to the War Memorial Opera House at all hours and want to be shown around. It is a famous place. The international conference that established the United Nations was held there; most of the mid-century's stars in opera, concert, symphony, and ballet have performed there, and something of their luster has mellowed its red plush seats and rubbed off on its travertine and gilt. The Opera House is a sight for West Coast tourists, and it has been carefully studied by numerous architects who have built similar theaters since 1932. It was necessary for someone to be there to do the honors. Julian Bagley saw the necessity for that someone even before the house was completed, and he convinced the trustees that he was the man for the job.

Over the years his function has expanded. It is typical of him that he had to make an appointment with the writer of these lines very late one afternoon, well after a symphony concert was over, because, he said, there were certain old ladies who depended on him alone to assist them into their cars. All the performers know him, of course, and his post-performance parties are legendary.

During those weeks when the War Memorial is dark or pre-empted by opera rehearsals, he sets out on pilgrimages to investigate opera houses elsewhere. There are few that he does not know, whether in the United States, Canada, or Europe. He has made three forays across the Atlantic on his quest, and now he is poised for his first invasion of Russia.

What has all this to do with the black man's folk tales? Nothing and everything. It is all part of a very rich personality, to whom music and the theater are essential, who knows the Louvre as well as he knows the Opéra, and who was a friend and fellow worker of such as Countee Cullen, James Weldon Johnson, and other writers involved in what used to be called the Negro Renaissance. *Candle-Lighting Time in Bodidalee* (accent on the "did") is by no means his first published effort, although it is his first book.

These are folk tales that Mr. Bagley heard as a child in and around the town of St. Nicholas, Florida, which is now a part of Jacksonville. His father was a shipyard worker, and he too worked in the shipyards for a time. He then went to Hampton Institute in Virginia for his education, graduated as an agriculturalist, and spent four years—1919 to 1922—as a district farm demonstration agent employed by the Department of Agriculture. His job was to help black farmers in Virginia to improve their methods, and in the process he swapped stories with them. He heard many of the tales of Bodidalee in Virginia, too; but the Virginia versions, he says, were tougher, more violent, and more in the tradition of the slave revolts that had racked that part of the world than in the easygoing tradition of Florida. Nevertheless, hearing the Virginia versions helped fix the stories in his mind, and he has been turning them all over in thought ever since. The tales in his book, it will be seen, grow more complex and interlocked as the book proceeds, and that is his contribution to them.

Mr. Bagley went to San Francisco in 1922, managed a hotel there for ten years—and the rest is Opera House history. Now he makes literary and folkloristic history as well. The author of this book has never been seen in the War Memorial without a red carnation in the buttonhole of his dark, discreet, and beautifully tailored coat. Much the same thing is to be said, metaphorically, of *Candle-Lighting Time in Bodidalee*.

Alfred V. Frankenstein

Introduction

A long time ago, in my native Florida, we young ones had a nice-sounding word that we loved to play around with. The nice-sounding word was *Bodidalee.*

Now there were many reasons why we enjoyed playing around with this word. But I think the one *big* reason was because it fitted so softly into our stories, sayings, and rhymes. To tell the truth, playing with it in such ways was like having a great big room full of building blocks with which we could make a marvelous little dream road to some faraway land of enchantment. Often we proclaimed, "She danced out her shoes all the way to Bodidalee!"

"Gone to Bodidalee. I mean really gone!"

Sometimes we even made up limping little rhymes about this imaginary place.

Where's Bodidalee,
Tell me, dear—
Is it far,
Or is it near?
Is it big—
Or is it small,
Or is it just a name to call?

Then some quick thinker among us, sitting in the house or picking oranges in the orange groves or walking along a dusty road—or maybe even fishing from a bateau on the river—would holler back,

Bodidalee big?—Bodidalee small?
Bodidalee's just a name to call!
Where's Bodidalee? Listen, dear,
Bodidalee's here, Bodidalee's there—
Bodidalee's almost everywhere!

Then there were the stories that the old folks had brought a long, long time ago from faraway Africa. My, how we did love to listen to and then retell these stories! But in retelling them, where do you suppose we said we had heard them? Why, in Bodidalee, of course. For in that here-there-almost-everywhere place we were tied down with no strings. With our imagination we could fly away into space. We could skip over high waves in the sea. We could burrow through the earth like ground moles plowing through ink-black soil in the middle of the night. Yes, indeed. In Bodidalee we could do anything. Anything at all.

Thus, although the Bodidalee of these little stories is down South in my native Florida, it could just as well be a Bodidalee of your own imagination, or away off somewhere like high up in the hills of New Hampshire. Or by the waters of Lake Michigan. Or far out in the Golden West, where the mountains run down to the sea. Or it could even be farther away, in Africa, where so many stories are told, and where the ones in this little book originated.

Yes, indeed. Believe me, Bodidalee can be anywhere. Anywhere at all.

Julian Bagley
Russian Hill
San Francisco,
California.

1

The Right Drumstick

With his eyes blinking like flashes of lightning and his ears bucked upright, Randy Rabbit, holding back a mouthful of laughter, slid the oven-warm turkey onto the table.

"Now we're ready to eat," said he to Bonee Bear, Wiley Wolf, and Fonee Fox. "Help yourselves!"

"But who's going to do the serving?" Bonee Bear asked.

"Why, Randy Rabbit, of course," said Wiley Wolf.

"No. Not I!" Randy Rabbit said, still blinking his eyes, bucking his ears, and sniffing the delicious odor of the oven-warm turkey. "Didn't I cook the bird? And isn't that enough?"

"But we went out and rustled up everything," Fonee Fox said. "Bonee Bear brought in the corn, Wiley Wolf fetched in the beans—and I snucked up on good old Mister Turkey."

"Yes, I know," Randy Rabbit said. "But didn't we all agree that I should stay home and rest up for the big job of cooking? And didn't all of you come back at moonrise

tired as young ones at bedtime? And didn't you sleep till
the sun was high up in the heavens? Of course you did.
But me—did I sleep late? Indeed I didn't. I was up at the
crack of dawn. Shucking corn. Stringing beans. Cleaning
and stuffing and roasting old Mister Turkey."

"By golly, that's right," old Bonee Bear said. "And
you've more than done your share."

"Then," said Randy Rabbit to Bonee Bear, "suppose, in

our choice for the carving, we honor someone else."

"How about Wiley Wolf?" said Fonee Fox.

"Right!" said Randy Rabbit, chuckling aloud.

"Now," thought Wiley Wolf, hiding his thoughts with a serious air, "I am sure of getting that right turkey drumstick, because it's bound to be hidden on the underside of the bird. And I mean to carve off meat for everybody else before I serve myself. Then I'll carve off that big old right drumstick. And I'll save it till tonight. Then I'll have the right to call the figures for the dancers at the big Corn Dance. And I'll get myself a whole load of love and hugs and kisses from some of the pretty gals there. And won't that be something to brag about!"

But as he picked up the carving knife he said kind of soft and low and innocent, "Now, Randy Rabbit, which part of the turkey do you fancy?"

"Oh, I'm choosy," Randy Rabbit said. "*Real choosy.* Any part suits me. Any part except the right drumstick. Because, you see, it wouldn't be polite for me to ask for that since I prepared the dinner and had a chance to cut it off long ago."

So, after a lengthy pause, Wiley Wolf sliced off a long, thin slice of white meat from the breast of Mister Turkey and shoveled it onto Randy Rabbit's plate. Then he said, "And what part will you choose, Fonee Fox?"

"I'll have a drumstick — but the right one, if you please!" Fonee Fox insisted.

"Oh, it doesn't matter about the right drumstick," Wiley Wolf laughed. "One's as good as the other."

"Right!" Randy Rabbit agreed.

"No, you're wrong," Fonee Fox said. "I want the right drumstick, because it will give me the right to call the figures at the big Corn Dance tonight. Then I can call to my side all the pretty girls there. And I can hug 'em and kiss 'em, and for a long, long spell, hold 'em in my arms.

Then I'll be a hero—envied, talked about, and loved for all the days to come by every girl in The Forest."

"All right, then," said Wiley Wolf, "if that's why you want it, let's give everyone a chance. I mean, let's draw straws for the favored drumstick and all this chance at kissing and loving and holding gals in your arms for such a long, long spell!"

"An excellent idea," said Bonee Bear.

"Fair enough," the others agreed.

Then they all drew straws.

"Ha! Ha! Ha!" laughed Wiley Wolf. "Oh, look, look, look! I've beat you all to it. See. I've got the longest straw. So now one of you will have to choose the left drumstick. Leaving it on this turkey after our big Thanksgiving Dinner just wouldn't seem right. Why, it might even give us all a spell of bad luck!"

For a moment no one said a word.

Wiley Wolf carved off the left drumstick and forked it onto Fonee Fox's plate. Then he said, "Now, of course, Bonee Bear, I reckon you're just like Fonee Fox. I mean, since you're unable to get the right drumstick, it really doesn't matter which part you choose. So I'm slicing off this choice bit of white meat for you. Right from the breast. See?"

Bonee Bear nodded his head. Then Wiley Wolf carved off a big piece of white breast meat and shoveled it onto Bonee Bear's plate. And once more he went on talking, "Old Mister Turkey is getting sorta slim. Reckon I'd better turn him over."

So, for the first time, Wiley Wolf flipped Mister Turkey over.

"Randy Rabbit," cried Fonee Fox, "where's that right drumstick?"

"Couldn't tell you if my head was off!" Randy Rabbit said.

"Very well," Wiley Wolf said. "Then let's go on with the dinner. But I'd bet a bushel of corn against a quart of tomatoes that Randy Rabbit has that right drumstick. Cut it off early this afternoon after he'd cooked the bird. We should have noticed that long ago. Who ever heard of a turkey laid right side down to be carved so's you could see only the left drumstick?"

"But," said Bonee Bear, "how could we pay attention to such matters when we were so hungry and the turkey smelled so good and we were so anxious to get on with the eating?"

"Yes, that's right," said Fonee Fox. "And since it's too late now for me to catch another bird and fetch it here and watch over Randy Rabbit while he cooks it, I guess tonight at the big Corn Dance it'll be up to me to get along with a left drumstick, eh?"

But no one ventured to answer Fonee Fox.

And so, in deep silence and suspicion, the rest of the meal was eaten.

Then night came and found them all at the big Corn Dance. And Randy Rabbit, full of mischief, shouted, "If any of you dancers had turkey today and have the right drumstick with you, you're entitled to call the figures for the dances tonight. Do you hear?"

"I've got a drumstick!" Fonee Fox hollered.

"I've got one, too!" Randy Rabbit hollered back. And sure enough, he reached under his coat and pulled out a great big turkey drumstick—the right one!

"Well, well!" someone sang out. "Hooray for Randy Rabbit—the lucky caller of the figures for the whirling and the swinging at the Corn Dance tonight!"

Poor old Wiley Wolf fairly shook with anger. But he could do nothing to help himself. So Randy Rabbit, in a great blaze of glory, strutted out onto the middle of the floor and commenced to call the figures. And every now

and then, and just to sort of soothe the anger of Wiley
Wolf, he would turn his attention to Fonee Fox, and he
would sing out numbers that would make Fonee Fox
switch to some girl he did not wish to dance with. Then,
just for pure devilment, he would holler out to Fonee Fox's
favorite girl, "Now come stand by the caller. Now put your
arms around him. Now give him a little kiss. Hooray! Now
give him another kiss. Tee-hee. Now double and triple the
kisses. Yum! Yum!"

All this, of course, sort of pleased Wiley Wolf. But it

made Fonee Fox shake with anger and shame. So when the dance was over, he grabbed Randy Rabbit by the ears and said, "Come with me, old Mister Fibber. We're going down by the riverside to the place where I caught that bird."

Pretty soon they were there. And sure enough, every single turkey, roosting and long asleep, had his right drumstick tucked up and completely out of sight.

Doubling up with laughter, little old Randy Rabbit said, "Aha. Look! Didn't I tell you Mister Turkey had no right drumstick?"

"But wait a while," Fonee Fox said as he frightened each turkey into putting down a right drumstick. "Look, look, look! Now what do you say to that?"

"Nothing," said Randy Rabbit. "You didn't say *shoo* to the one on the table today. If you had, he would've put down a right drumstick, too. But you didn't say *shoo* like you've just this moment said. See?"

Then Randy Rabbit was gone, rushing off into the first soft light of the breaking dawn. Poor little old Fonee Fox, alone and still gazing at the turkeys standing there before him on both legs, could only hear, coming back to him in faint and fainter echoes, "But you didn't say *shoo*—see!"

2

The
High-Low
Jump

Stealing that right drumstick and the chance to call the
figures at the Corn Dance Thanksgiving Night had made
Randy Rabbit mighty biggity and sassy and sure of himself. But that wasn't all. It had given him the urge to steal
whenever he was hungry, with perfect confidence that he
wouldn't be caught.

So every night that summer he would sneak into some
farmer's garden, bite big plugs from ripe tomatoes, nip
off the heads of nice green lettuce, and gnaw on ever so
many ears of growing corn. Sometimes, on a very hot
night, he'd bite even bigger plugs from the tomatoes and
let the cool juice drip down over his head. Then he'd say
to himself, "My, but that feels good. So nice and cool!"

Then he'd skip away, laughing, all full of joy and cool-
ness, to make merry of his big feed to his good friend
Bonee Bear.

"Well," he'd say, "I just came here to tell you about the good feed that I've just had in old Farmer Brown's garden. I bet I plugged more than a dozen ripe tomatoes there. And I must have gnawed on at least that many ears of corn. Nipped off the heads of lots of lettuce, too. And it was all done because I was very, very hungry and mighty clever and sure no one could catch and punish me."

20

When he could stand no more of such sure and sassy talk, Bonee Bear would say, "Listen, Randy Rabbit. That's too much eating at one time for anybody, and one of these days you will crave some of the very things that you now waste by overstuffing yourself. Especially corn. Yessiree. Mark my word. You're going to want just as sure's you're born. Look at me. I steal from the farmers too — especially corn. But do I waste it like you? No. You bet your life I don't. I store it up for the lean winter days. And that's exactly what you should do. No fooling. Believe me, Randy Rabbit, you should take some thought of tomorrow. You should use your head. Use it for something else besides holding your big ears apart."

"Ha! Ha!" Randy Rabbit would chuckle. "Me want? Why, Bonee Bear, have you gone plumb crazy?"

Then Bonee Bear would hush his mouth and say no more.

But Randy Rabbit would keep right on boasting, "I have never, *never* wanted for food in my life, Bonee Bear. And I never shall."

"All right," Bonee Bear would say. "Don't pay me no mind. Don't listen to me at all. But when you're cold and hungry and wanting, don't come a-running to my door with your misery."

"Don't worry, I won't," Randy Rabbit would say. And once more, as soon as it was night again, he would dash off to the gardens down by the riverside.

Then winter came. And one night when Randy Rabbit was very hungry and searching for a morsel to eat, he met Fonee Fox and cried out loud, "I'm starving. I'm starving. Where can I find some food? Tomatoes. Corn. Anything at all."

"Aren't you and Bonee Bear the best of friends?" said Fonee Fox.

"Sure," said Randy Rabbit.

"Very well, then," said Fonee Fox, "go and ask him for some corn. He's got plenty."

"Oh, my good gracious, no," said Randy Rabbit. "I just don't have the nerve to beg off Bonee Bear."

"Then," argued Fonee Fox in his soft, smooth, persuasive way, "if you don't have the nerve to ask your best of friends for corn, how do you expect to get it?"

"I don't know," Randy Rabbit said.

Sly old Fonee Fox went on, "Well, now, as for me, I don't really need any corn. But all the same, if I had some, I could use it to trap that fat old hen that cackles around my place every day. So if you've just got to have food tonight, Randy Rabbit, come along with me to Bonee Bear's corncrib. We're sure of finding enough there to last us through the winter."

The two prowlers went off into the night. When they came to the end of their journey and heard Bonee Bear snoring loudly—in his bed, a little way from his corncrib— Fonee Fox whispered to Randy Rabbit, "Now we're all set. Look. Since I'm heavier than you, I'll use this pry pole. I'll poke it between the logs of the corncrib. Then I'll sit down on it till I've made a hole big enough for you to jump through. Then you can pitch out all the corn we need— and scramble right back through the same opening you squeezed in by. Because I'll keep it wide open by sitting tight till you're out. See? Then we'll have our corn. And Bonee Bear, still snoring his old fat hips off, will never know who robbed him. Understand?"

"Sure," said Randy Rabbit.

Delighted, Fonee Fox leaped on the pry pole and forced a big gap between the logs of the crib. Little old Randy Rabbit scrambled through and began pitching out the corn.

Instantly awakened by the noise, old Bonee Bear stumbled from his bed and came tramping toward the corncrib, sniffing, snorting, puffing, blowing.

Without a moment's warning, Fonee Fox leaped off the pry pole and dashed away. Poor little Randy Rabbit! There he was—shut up in the corncrib. His heart pounded like thunder. His throat went dry. His ears trembled. And in the long suspense of his waiting, he counted off a lifetime. Then he began to search for some secret nook or cranny in

which he could hide. But alas, the floor of the crib offered none. And old Bonee Bear, still restless and suspicious, kept sniffing about and tramping around the place where his food was stored.

Just as Randy Rabbit was about to scream aloud and give himself up, he saw, in the little ribbon of moonlight trickling in above him, the very spot he had been looking for.

He made one big leap, and there he was—high on a board, just above the doorsill of the corncrib. At that very moment old Bonee Bear, plunging his weight against the door, came stumbling in.

Down to the floor Randy Rabbit leaped, landing with his face pressed hard against the outer side of the door.

"Howdy!" he said to Bonee Bear. Then pushing himself inside, he went on, "Came around to help you shuck some corn. Heard you were looking for help. Got the news from Fonee Fox. But he's such a fibber. You can't believe a thing he says. All the same, I thought I'd come round late tonight—when I was sure of catching you in—and see for myself. Say—look—do you really need some corn-shucking help?"

"Indeed I don't!" said Bonee Bear with a loud and loony laugh. "Long ago I shucked all the corn I need."

Then he pushed the little intruder from the corncrib.

"Don't get the idea that I'm really hungry!" Randy Rabbit flung back at him. "Indeed I'm not. Why, you old bag of fat, I'm just now beginning to enjoy the tomatoes and lettuce and corn that I barely tasted last summer!"

Then he ran home, trotting all the way to the convincing little jingle that he'd made up on the spot:

Now you've got your belly full,
Sleep will come as soft as wool,
As soft as wool, as soft as wool,
Sleep will come as soft as wool!

3

The Bamboo Cutter

"Hello there, Randy Rabbit!" said Fonee Fox. "How do you do this morning?"

"Poorly. Poorly," said Randy Rabbit, making no mention of being left by Fonee Fox in Bonee Bear's corncrib the night before. "I'm no count. I'm all in. I'm shaky and woozy and all in from hunger."

"Then why go about in such a condition?" Fonee Fox asked.

"Well, I'm going to the river to meet my old friend, Mister Tortoise," Randy Rabbit said.

"But you'll starve down there, too," Fonee Fox said. "I myself have just come from a long-time fishing trip to the river. I caught nothing. And so far your friend Mister Tortoise has caught only a little minnow fish—scarcely big enough to feed a fly."

"But you should have stayed till the tide changed,"

Randy Rabbit said. "That's when the fish bite."

"No," said Fonee Fox. "It was too cold down there for me. All the same, I've promised to go back before sundown to fetch home your friend and his big load of fish. But I have no intention of returning to that cold spot. Instead, I'm going up the hill to Mister Tortoise's den—if I can find it."

Then, for a moment, Fonee Fox was silent. But he soon came back to the point of his plan and said, "Say—look here, Randy Rabbit. It seems to me you ought to know where Mister Tortoise lives. Come on now. Out with it."

"Sure I know," Randy Rabbit said. "But if you propose to rob him of the food that he's stored up for the winter, then I'll keep where he lives a secret, thank you!"

"And still you say you're hungry?" Fonee Fox said.

"Yes—starving!" said Randy Rabbit.

"Then," said Fonee Fox, "will you listen to a scheme that will get us both a big feed?"

"Yes," Randy Rabbit promised.

"Good. More than good," Fonee Fox said. "This is it. While Mister Tortoise is down at the river fishing, we will go to his den and rob him of a fine meal of carrots and beets and turnips. Do you see?"

27

"Oh, no, no!" Randy Rabbit cried. "A thousand times no! Why, Mister Tortoise is my friend. I could never pull a trick like that on him."

"But how's he going to know?" argued Fonee Fox. "Isn't he down by the riverside fishing? Of course he is. Right there where I just left him a little while ago."

"Fonee Fox, I've made up my mind to go along with you," Randy Rabbit finally declared. "Wait here till I run home and fetch us a basket. We'll need it to put the food in—don't you think?"

"Sure," said Fonee Fox. Then Randy Rabbit was gone.

But on his way home Randy Rabbit began thinking of how last night, at the first sign of danger, Fonee Fox had leaped off the safety pry pole and left him trapped in Bonee Bear's corncrib. Then he thought of all the favors that Mister Tortoise had done for him. And so, before he'd run halfway to his own grounds, he whirled around and raced back to the river.

"Oh, my good gracious!" Mister Tortoise cried. "You almost scared the daylights out o' me. Where'd you come from?"

"From up the road a piece," Randy Rabbit said. "And I've just been talking with Fonee Fox."

"Sure enough," Mister Tortoise said. "And what did the sly old rascal have to say?"

"Said he'd been down here all morning fishing with you.

Said you'd only caught a little minnow fish. Said . . ."

But before Randy Rabbit could finish, Mister Tortoise asked, "Did that good-for-nothing rascal say that I promised him something to eat?"

"Yes," said Randy Rabbit. "But now he plans to steal all you've got. That's what we talked about. He tried to coax me into showing him your den. He wanted to rob it."

"The low-down scamp!" Mister Tortoise cried. "Just imagine anyone trying to pull a trick like that on a good friend!"

"But," Randy Rabbit went on, "I've thought of a plan that'll put the old scalawag to shame. Now you just listen. To give me strength, I'll eat this little minnow fish you have here. Then you'll hop on my back and let me take you to your den. Then I'll go back and get Fonee Fox and fetch him there. Then I'll pretend I'm going to steal your carrots and beets and turnips. But I'll fool him into letting me stay on guard at the entrance of your place. And when he sneaks down to where you're hiding, you'll grab him by the neck. And when you're done with him, he will never darken your door again. See?"

Mister Tortoise, nodding his head, agreed to everything. Then the two sure-enough friends, the one on the back of the other, were off.

In a little while the journey ended. And Mister Tortoise, sliding from Randy Rabbit's back, scrambled down into his den to wait for Fonee Fox.

In the meantime Randy Rabbit raced back to meet the enemy.

"I just couldn't find the basket," he said as he strolled into view. "Looked hard for it, though. No luck. Just a wasted bit of time."

"But how come you are panting so hard?" said Fonee Fox.

"I don't know," Randy Rabbit said.

"Hush your mouth," said Fonee Fox. "You're nothing but a mush-mouth fibber. Long before you arrived, strolling along so slow and easy and innocent, I heard you away back yonder, a-running through the swamp—*bookiter! bookiter! bookiter!* And how come your breath smells so much like fish? A little minnow fish? *You couldn't find the basket. Looked hard for it, though. Everywhere.* Now did you ever, in all your born days, hear such awful fibbing?"

Well, there was no doubt about it. Fonee Fox knew what he was talking about. But he was so hungry, and the part played by Randy Rabbit, though unconvincing, was so soft and calm and easy that he decided to take the risk of going along with him to rob Mister Tortoise's den.

But when he arrived and saw all the fresh tracks around the hole, he balked and declared, "No! No, Randy Rabbit! I will never take such a chance. It isn't worth it. Why, at this very moment Mister Tortoise might be down there waiting for me."

"Then *I'll* go down," Randy Rabbit said. "You stay here and I'll fill the pockets of my suit with food and bring it along with me."

Then Randy Rabbit slid down to the bottom of the den to join Mister Tortoise.

"We've got to think up a better trick than our first one," he said. "Fonee Fox is awfully suspicious."

"Just leave it to me," Mister Tortoise said. "And when I tell you to squeal—squeal with all your might. And when I tell you to lie down and play dead—lie down and play dead. Understand?"

"Yes," Randy Rabbit whispered. And at that very moment Mister Tortoise seized him and pretended that one great and mighty scuffle was going on below.

And old Fonee Fox, away up at the entrance to the den, trembled with excitement.

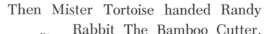

Then Mister Tortoise handed Randy Rabbit The Bamboo Cutter. Then he directed him to one corner of the den.

"Now lie down," he whispered. "Pretend you are dead. And when I holler 'The Bamboo Cutter!' you leap up and dash to my side."

"Wonderful!" said Randy Rabbit.

"Hey, down there," Fonee Fox shouted. "What's happened? Are you all right, Randy Rabbit? Are you all right? Hello. Hello. Hello, down there! Randy Rabbit, are you all right? Hello. Hello. Hello, down there!"

"Who's that up there darkening my den?" Mister Tortoise finally called out.

"Why, it's me," Fonee Fox answered. "Your friend. I've come for the carrots and beets and turnips you promised me down by the riverside this morning? Remember?"

"Sure I remember,"

Mister Tortoise said. "Come on down. But say, aren't you
the lucky one to arrive when I've just killed a nice fat
rabbit! Hurry up. Come on down and help me skin him,
and you shall have a nice piece of fresh meat to go with
your vegetables."

So, shameless and with great joy, Fonee Fox slid down
to the bottom of the den and began strutting around and
smacking his lips.

"The Bamboo Cutter!" Mister Tortoise shouted. "The
Bamboo Cutter! Come quick. Come quick with The Bamboo Cutter!"

And Randy Rabbit, leaping to his feet, dashed forward
with the weapon, a bamboo reed with frightful, sawlike
teeth cut into it.

"The Bamboo Cutter! The Bamboo Cutter!" Mister Tortoise called out again and again as he tightened his grip on Fonee Fox. "Draw it across his throat, Randy Rabbit. Draw it across his throat till his head falls off."

And by now poor old Fonee Fox, feeling the frightful sawlike teeth of The Bamboo Cutter jagging across his throat, shook with terror.

He ducked his head left. He ducked his head right. He kicked. He spat. He hissed. He groaned. He grunted. He gnashed his teeth. And the white foam in the corners of his mouth flew in every direction.

"Oh, I'm dead! I'm dead!" he finally screamed.

"Shut up your mouth," Mister Tortoise teased. "Did a dead fox ever hear himself holler?"

Then, smiling and winking at Randy Rabbit, he went on teasing and poking fun at Fonee Fox, "If we let him go now, are you sure his head will drop off as he runs away?"

"Sure I'm sure," said Randy Rabbit.

"Then," shouted Mister Tortoise, "let him be up and off and away to a grave as bloody as his shall be!"

And so, still shaking with terror, he leaped to his feet, and before Mister Tortoise or Randy Rabbit could even say *Boo,* he was gone.

4

Old Mister Smoothback

A long time ago, by the banks of the river at the edge of The Forest, there lived a big and fierce old crocodile. And this was the first crocodile in the river. Before him there were no others. And he lived very secluded in a big cluster of thick brush. Although many other, much larger creatures lived there, this old Mister Crocodile was king of them all. And what a cruel king he was! Every day some poor unfortunate one was seized and crushed to death between his mighty, savage, saw-teeth jaws.

He was very fond of frogs, and every day he would crush dozens of them to death. The frogs, to be sure, could hop faster than Mister Crocodile could run or swim, and in a fair race he never caught them. But, of course, this mean old rascal's way of playing the game of life and death was never fair. He simply lay hidden in the mud, waiting for some poor little frog to come paddling along. Then he would seize and crush him to death between his mighty, savage, saw-teeth jaws.

But at that time old Mister Crocodile's back was very smooth and black, and it was very easy for him to hide in the brush and mud.

One day, however, Mister Bullfrog, who was king and daddy of all the little frogs, raced down to the riverside and said, "I've just been talking with Randy Rabbit, and he declares that the only way to stop this murder of our little ones is for us to pile up little lumps of mud on old Mister Crocodile's back. Then, says Randy Rabbit, we can always tell where our cruel enemy lies."

"Right!" croaked the littlest frog.

"More than right!" the others sang.

So the next time old Mister Crocodile crawled into the mud for his long winter nap, Mister Bullfrog and all the other little frogs in the river at the edge of The Forest

hopped to the place where the monster lay. Then they began dabbing a thousand piles of mud dabs on his back. And when they had finished the job, lo and behold, Mister Crocodile could be seen from any part of the riverside.

"Now we're safe," Mister Bullfrog grunted.

"Right!" croaked the littlest frog.

"More than right!" the others sang.

Then they all joined hands, formed a big circle around the sleeping crocodile, and while Mister Bullfrog beat time on his knee, the others, with throats puffed out like little rubber balls, sang a cute little jingle. And the cute little jingle said that now, with the mud piles stuck on his back, it made no difference where Mister Crocodile lay, they could find him any day.

How happy they all were! Time and again the cute little song was shouted. And when they sang it the last time, Mister Bullfrog got so happy that he stopped beating on his knee, leaped into the air, spun around like a top, landed, danced a jig, and then chorused in with the others. And his big, booming bass voice echoed along the riverside like a whole flock of people clapping hands in a great, big, room-sized jug. And he sang out loud above all the others,

Ho, Mister Crocodile, king for a while,
Fixed up now in fine, fine style,
Anywhere you choose to lie,
We can spot you with the eye!

Then the singing and dancing were over, and all the frogs, except Mister Bullfrog, returned to their homes to await the awakening of Mister Crocodile.

Winter passed, then it was spring.

Mister Crocodile made one loud and thundering sound, and all the little frogs came racing to the riverside to join Mister Bullfrog. Fascinated, they stood glued to the earth while Mister Crocodile groaned and bellowed like a full-

grown bull. He flapped his tail. And he shook his back like
a puppy trying to shake off a whole mess of biting fleas.
But the more he went in for this carrying on, the madder
he became and the harder the little lumps of mud clung
to his old back.

Finally he swam ashore. He was hungry, mighty hungry,
and he looked everywhere for a morsel of food. Surely, he
told himself, there's a little frog about somewhere ashore.

But he was wrong. He could find nothing. Nothing at
all, for all the little frogs were safely hidden.

So he slipped back into the muddy waters of the river to see if he could sneak up on some poor little frogs. But in this also he failed, for no longer could he hide himself. Now, no matter how much his skin resembled the dark, muddy waters near the shores, the happy little frogs could always tell where he lay by the big black bumps they'd stuck onto his back.

5

Lookit
the
Little Pig!

The Little Papa Pig and the Little Mama Pig thought they had everything their hearts could wish for, and they were very happy until that day when Randy Rabbit came along and said, "Look. You have a pretty nice and cozy place here. But you need a cover over your pen because in a little while the rains will be coming. Then if you've no protection, you'll be drowned in the downpour."

"Maybe he's right," the Little Mama Pig said as Randy Rabbit went on skipping down the road.

So the next morning, when the farmer who owned them came out to feed them, the Little Papa Pig said, "Oh, Mister Farmer-man, won't you please give us a cover for our pen?"

"Why, certainly," promised the Farmer-man. "Why didn't you ask me for one long ago?"

Well, this was mighty smooth talk. But all the same, it

put no cover over the little pigs' pen. Then pretty soon, sure enough, just like Randy Rabbit had said, a big rain came. And all that day it fell on the little pigs' faces. Then came night, darkness, and some let-up in the rain.

"You stay here," the Little Papa Pig said to the Little Mama Pig. "I'm going out to see if I can find something to make a cover for our pen."

Then he kissed his little darling good-by, leaped from the pen, and was on his way. By now there was a big silver moon, almost as bright as the noonday sun, to guide him. He hadn't gone far before he came to a big clump of palmettos.

"Ah-hah!" he thought, as he began gnawing at the stems. "These are just what I'm looking for."

And almost before he knew it, he'd cut down enough to serve his purpose. Then he headed for home.

When she saw him coming, the Little Mama Pig squealed with delight. But the Little Papa Pig threw down his load of palmettos and whispered, "Come now, hush! Don't you know carrying on like that will wake the Farmer-man? And remember we have to be done before he gets up. So we gotta keep moving. Understand?"

So all that night the Little Papa Pig and the Little Mama Pig worked at top speed. And when the Farmer-man came out in the morning to feed them he got the shock of his life.

"Tell me," he said, "who made the cover for your pen?"

"We did," the Little Papa Pig said. "Made it ourselves. Me and the Little Mama Pig."

"Did you really?" the Farmer-man said. "Well, you've certainly made yourselves the nicest, neatest, prettiest cover that ever shaded a pen. Why, it makes your place almost as nice and neat and pretty as mine."

Then the Farmer-man went away.

But pretty soon he came back roaring like a lion. Overnight someone had robbed his cornfield.

"Little Papa Pig," he shouted, "it was you who wrecked my cornfield last night! Get out! Get out! I don't want you any more. Wouldn't have you now if you were the last Little Papa Pig in the whole wide world. Yes, get out and rustle and root for yourself as long as ever you live!"

Of course the Little Papa Pig was not guilty of wrecking the cornfield. But after the fearful fuss of the Farmer-man, he thought it best to leave. So, with tears as big as raindrops in his eyes, he kissed the Little Mama Pig, leaped from the pen, and ran away.

And he hadn't been running too long before he came to

the same clump of palmettos from which he had built the marvelous cover over his pen. So he got another load of the little palms and hurried down to the riverside to build himself a house. And it was there, near the edge of the river, that he came upon Mister Crocodile cooling himself in the shade of a big palm tree.

"Oh, hello there, Little Pig," said Mister Crocodile. "What in the world are you doing with that great big load of palmettos? Why, you've got almost enough there to cool off everybody down by the riverside."

"But I'm not going to cool off anyone," the Little Papa Pig said. "I'm going to build myself a house."

"A house? Oh, I see," said Mister Crocodile. "But before you do that, won't you please fan me just a wee bit? I'm almost dead of the heat."

The Little Papa Pig said nothing.

"Oh, come on," Mister Crocodile pleaded. "Quit your trembling. Don't be afraid. I won't hurt you. It's all a fib about crocodiles swallowing little pigs alive. Or leaping on their backs and riding them madly till they finally fall and die of excitement and fright. Come on now. Fan me just a wee bit, won't you? Then I'll show you a nice cool place to build your house. What do you say—all right?"

"Yes," the Little Papa Pig said.

Then he came very close to Mister Crocodile and began cooling him off with one of the little palms.

"That feels *so good!*" Mister Crocodile said.

"I'm glad," the Little Papa Pig said. "It feels kinda good to me, too."

Then, by and by, when he was plenty cooled from being fanned and greatly refreshed by the little cat naps he'd taken, Mister Crocodile opened his eyes and began chatting about this, that, and the other.

"Not a bad fellow at all," the Little Papa Pig thought. Then he mentioned his bad luck with the Farmer-man.

"Well!" said Mister Crocodile. "So the Farmer-man thinks it was you who stole his corn last night, eh?"

"Yes," the Little Papa Pig said.

"Gosh," said Mister Crocodile, "never in his life has that farmer been so wrong. Why, it was Bonee Bear who stole that corn. I know. Didn't I see him passing by here late last night with his arms full? And right this moment, if it wasn't so awfully hot, I'd take you up the road a piece and show you some of the corn silks he dropped on his way home."

"That's good news," the Little Papa Pig said. "Now I can run home and tell the Farmer-man. Then maybe he'll let me come back to my nice little covered pen and the

Little Mama Pig. I'm awfully lonely without her. And I'll bet she's awfully lonely without me, too."

"But you mustn't go back right away," Mister Crocodile warned. "Wait a while. I want to set a trap for old Bonee Bear, and I'm wondering if you'll help me."

"Sure," the Little Papa Pig said. "I will do anything you say. Anything at all."

"Then, tonight," said Mister Crocodile, "you shall go to the Farmer-man's cornfield. Stay there till Bonee Bear shows up for his next load of corn. Then you must run as fast as you can toward the river. Naturally, he will try to catch you. But I'll meet you halfway up the road, and I'll trip the old smartie and teach him a lesson or two."

"Good!" the Little Papa Pig said.

"You know, Little Pig," Mister Crocodile went on, "I never did like old Bonee Bear. Besides being the thief who'll even steal eggs from an alligator's nest, he's also the one who pokes fun at my back. Says the rough, ugly bumps on it are little lumps of dried mud that were put there long ago by Mister Bullfrog and his gang."

Sitting in the cornfield that night, the Little Papa Pig did not wait too long before old Bonee Bear came in and began snapping off the ears of corn.

Rip! Rip!

Rip, rip, rip!

Then his arms were full.

Up jumped the Little Papa Pig.

Down tumbled Bonee Bear's load of corn.

Both took off for the river. The Little Papa Pig, in the lead, was running with all his might. Old Bonee Bear, close behind him, was running with all his might too. And what an awful thundering noise he was making as his big feet pounded the ground. On and on toward the river the two sped. And every now and then old Bonee Bear would get just close enough to the Little Papa Pig to swipe him with his big rough paws.

Then they were at the halfway mark. But old Mister Crocodile, tired of waiting, had given up the watch and gone back to the river. So the Little Papa Pig had to put

on more speed and keep on running toward the stream.

And when he was in sight of the water, panting desperately and wondering if he could possibly hold out a moment longer—with old Bonee Bear's big, rough paws swiping at him and plunging him forward with greater and greater speed—Mister Crocodile poked his head up from the river and hollered, "Oh, lookit the Little Pig. Come on, there. You can make it. You can make it to the river. Keep moving. Keep moving. Run, Little Pig. Run! Run! Run!"

And the Little Papa Pig, with his ears flat against his

head, his tail flying straight behind him, and his eyes bulging with fear, certainly was getting over some ground. To tell the truth, he scarcely seemed to touch the earth at all as in the clear moonlight the great clouds of dust whirled backward and screened him off from old Bonee Bear.

Then he plunged into the river.

And right after him leaped Bonee Bear, landing square in the clutches of Mister Crocodile, who ducked and held him under water till bubbles as big as baseballs whirled up from all his gasping.

"Stop it. Please stop it!" the Little Papa Pig cried. "You've punished him enough."

So, old Bonee Bear, now senseless and harmless, was pushed ashore. He rolled back and forth and up and over and over and up and into his senses again. Then he leaped to his feet, and with the water still gurgling in his stomach, dashed away. And the Little Papa Pig, thanking Mister Crocodile, dashed away too. But he was not, like Bonee Bear, running away to freedom in The Forest. Indeed he was not. He was speeding with all his might toward home, and the forgiveness of the old Farmer-man, and the love of the Little Mama Pig, and those dream-soft nights when the rain would tap ever so softly on his wonderful palmetto roof.

6

The Little Pig's Way Out

After Mister Crocodile had scared the daylights out of
Bonee Bear in the river that night and had saved the
Little Papa Pig's life, every bear in The Forest near the
riverside had it in for Mister Crocodile. So, of course,
whenever he crawled out from the river and lay on the
shore to sun himself, he had to watch out for danger—
very real danger. For all the bears of the great clan were
out to get him. They didn't care about catching the Little
Papa Pig, but they certainly did want to catch Mister
Crocodile.

It wasn't very long before he found this out and decided
to take action against the danger. Sometime soon, he was
sure, he would tell his friend, the clever Little Papa Pig,
about the trouble. But, at the moment, he dared not leave
the river, because if he did, the bears, he thought, would
most certainly nab him.

One day, however, he made up his mind to leave the
water. But at that very moment he looked up the road
and saw them coming—Bonee Bear and The Smart One.
He ducked his head under the water and lay perfectly
still. Then, while the bears lapped up a drink, he caught
snatches of their conversation.

"Oh, yes," said the one who was Bonee Bear, "one
of these days we shall most certainly nab that old Mister
Crocodile. We're as sure of getting him as we're sure of
getting our winter corn."

And when they had finished drinking, they lay down by the river to rest and talk further of their plan to catch Mister Crocodile. From what was said, it was clear that the whole scheme had been laid out by Bonee Bear and The Smart One, who had just drunk with him.

"Every day we'll keep on the watch down here," Bonee Bear vowed. "And if ever Mister Crocodile comes out for his sunning, we'll nab him. Then we'll holler for all the other bears to come and help us kill him."

Poor Mister Crocodile! For days, by struggling desperately, he managed to keep his head under water. But he knew that soon he would have to come up for a bit of air and the daytime light.

So again he thought of his friend, the Little Papa Pig. Surely he could find a way out for him. So that night, when Bonee Bear and The Smart One were off guard, he crawled from the water and made the journey.

"Hello there," he called out to the Little Papa Pig, who was climbing onto the top rail of his pen. "How are you? It's sure good to see you again. And it's wonderful to see the Little Mama Pig for the first time. What a darling! No wonder you were so anxious to get back to her that night.

But tell me, how is the palmetto roof working? Does it
keep out the sun and rain?"

"Very well indeed," the Little Papa Pig said. "But tell
me about yourself. How're things moving?"

"Fine and dandy," Mister Crocodile said. "But what do
you think of this? The bears in The Forest have all heard
about my saving your life. They know, too, that I scared
the daylights out of Bonee Bear that night in the river.

So they're plotting to kill me. They don't want you. Said so down by the river. But they'd give the world for me.

"Now, Little Pig," Mister Crocodile went on, "I did all I could to help you out of a tight place. What are you going to do to help me? You know how it is with me. I've just got to have sunshine. And I can't possibly get it with Bonee Bear and The Smart One on guard at the river all day. So tell me, please—you've talked with Randy Rabbit a lot—isn't there some way out?"

"Indeed there is!" the Little Papa Pig said.

Then they heard a heavy tramping down the road.

"It's Bonee Bear and The Smart One, searching for me!" Mister Crocodile cried.

"Climb in and hide," the Little Papa Pig said.

Loping up to the pen, Bonee Bear and The Smart One sniffed around a time or two, snatched and scratched at the top rail, then galloped away, sure of their enemy's hiding place. Shaking crazily, Mister Crocodile said nothing.

But presently the moon came up and shone on a big, bright, and golden idea. Out in the field, near the little pigs' pen, stood a scarecrow. It had been put there by the Farmer-man to scare the crows away.

"Oh—look, look!" the Little Papa Pig cried, pointing to his golden idea. "Listen. We're going to take those clothes off that old scarecrow and we're going to dress you up like a natural man. Understand?"

"Yes," Mister Crocodile said.

Then the Little Papa Pig and the Little Mama Pig began dressing him up. They took off the old scarecrow's suit and put it on Mister Crocodile. Then they pulled the old derby hat down over his eyes, shoved the scarecrow's wooden gun under one arm, added a touch here and there, and before he knew it Mister Crocodile looked like a sure-enough man!

"Now," said Mister Crocodile, "what shall I do?"

"Keep holding that gun like a real bad man," the Little
Papa Pig said. "And that derby hat, for goodness sake,
keep it pulled down over your eyes. Then if you should
meet Bonee Bear and The Smart One on your return to
the river, they'll never know you. But you'd better mind.
Keep moving. Keep a level head. Don't get nervous. If
you show the least signs of being afraid, they will certainly find you out."

Well, everything went along just fine and dandy until
Mister Crocodile, halfway on his journey, came face to
face with Bonee Bear and The Smart One. Then, in spite
of the Little Papa Pig's solemn warning, he began trembling all over. He was scared stiff. But Bonee Bear and
The Smart One were trembling and much afraid, too.

So it was Mister Crocodile who kept the best head. He kept on advancing, his wooden gun raised like a real bad man's. And it happened: Bonee Bear and The Smart One galloped away in panics of fright and a great cloud of dust as high as the moon, leaving Mister Crocodile glued to his tracks and shaking with a fit of uncontrollable laughter.

Then, with a firm, brave step and his laughter under control, he strode on down to the river, where, in the moonlight on the shore, he rigged the scarecrow on a tree—with gun, derby hat, and all—and left it there forever more to scare the bears away.

7

The Great Fishbowl Contest

How long Mister Crocodile had been in the river at the edge of The Forest, no one knew. Nor did anyone know where he'd come from. Some of the old folks said he had been blown in on a hurricane from faraway Africa. Others said he'd come from a buzzard egg hatched by the sun.

But one thing was sure: he was in the river now, and he'd been there for a long, long time. And most of the time he'd been happy, free, and full of mischief, and not the least bit lonely. Then, to scare the bears away, he had rigged up that scarecrow down by the riverside. And the scarecrow had worked out fine. Too fine. For not only had it scared the bears away, it had scared away the crows and hawks and robins and larks. And there was no life down by the riverside. Mister Crocodile was lonely. Very lonely.

"This is awful," he thought. "I will cry out for a mate.

I can no longer stand this awful loneliness."

Then he sent out a long, lonely call.

But when the young Miss Gator, answering his call, arrived, she saw right away that she was very different from Mister Crocodile. And she told him so.

"I'm sorry," she said. "I could never be your mate. My kinsmen, the alligators, would never accept you. You're too different from us. Your head is slenderer. Your teeth project from the sides of your mouth. And your eyes are fierce and wild. And the moment they saw you they would shout,

He's as different from Beau Gator
As an orange is from a tater!
Different! Different! Different!

Then she went off to return to her kinsmen in The Great Fishbowl.

But Mister Crocodile was not discouraged. Night after night, he sent out a call. A very lonely call. "I'm lonesome and sad and blue," it said. "Please come and be my mate."

But no mate came. So, by and by, he went out and found the young Miss Gator of the long-ago visit.

"I've come," he said, "to make you a serious offer. A lonely offer of love. At the time of the full moon, I hear, there'll be a contest held in The Great Fishbowl. They say all the alligators from the river will be there, and I wish to come and try my skill at pitching fish into the shell-ringed circle. If I should win, I hear that I may have the choice of any young Miss Gator in the Bowl, and I hope you'll let me choose you. May I come and try?"

"Yes," she said.

And so, on the night of the full moon and The Great Fishbowl Contest, the lonely Mister Crocodile found himself facing the great herd of strange creatures. And here was his opponent, the young Beau Gator. And just as the young Miss Gator had warned, all these strange creatures were shouting in loud and hostile voices,

He's as different from Beau Gator,
As an orange is from a tater!
Different! Different! Different!

But Mister Crocodile was not afraid, for now he had his mind set only on winning the young Miss Gator.

So he strode forward.

From the great pile of fish stacked in the bottom of the Bowl he selected a round, fat one. He tossed it toward the shell-ringed circle.

It missed.

Then young Beau Gator had his turn.

He, too, missed his mark.

But neither of these turns counts for much, said the great circle of alligators, because each fish has been tossed with the forepaws. Now Mister Crocodile and young Beau Gator will have to toss a winner with their mouths.

But again, each missed the mark.

"Now remember," Mister Crocodile heard them shout,

"in The Great Fishbowl Contest, it is neither the forepaws nor the mouths that count. It's the tails! Why, even in the river, isn't it with the deadly aim of the tails that fish are knocked into the mouths of Beau Gator and Mister Crocodile?"

"Sure!" All heads in the Bowl nodded.

There was a chorus of honks for Mister Crocodile as the first fish, flipped with the tail, landed in the center of the shell-ringed circle.

But Beau Gator's fish flipped with the tail landed there, too. And so did the second, third, and fourth ones of both contestants.

"Come on!" everybody grumbled. "Get going! You're both taking it too easy."

So Mister Crocodile and Beau Gator tried again. Into the air glided a little sand dab from Beau Gator's side. It landed right in the center of the little shell-ringed circle.

Into the air one shot from Mister Crocodile's side, and it, too, sailed back and landed in the center of the little shell-ringed circle.

And so each contestant went on like this, pitching fish with the tail, sometimes landing them in the center of the circle and sometimes missing.

Then the score was tied and Beau Gator had had his last chance, and now Mister Crocodile came up for his final fling.

He leaned forward. He aimed carefully. And with his tail, he gave the little sand dab a violent whack. Up and far into the air it sailed, flashing in the moonlight like a silver dish.

Then, for a moment, it paused, darted crazily down, landed in the center of The Winner's Circle, and sent Mister Crocodile and the young Miss Gator strutting from The Great Fishbowl Contest fairly bubbling over with happiness.

8

The River-Road Ramble

So there he was, poor Mister Crocodile, trapped all alone in a bamboo cage, high up in The Forest and miles and miles from his beloved ones and the river.

He glanced about him. Only the tiny openings in the heavy bamboo meshes of his cage met his eyes.

"But they're too small to squeeze through," he thought.

Then he cocked his head and caught the early morning sun streaming in through the uncovered top of his cage.

"Ah!" he thought. "Surely this is the way out. For I can easily leap to freedom over this uncovered top. Then I can race back to the river and search for my beloved ones."

He limbered up. He spun around crazily on the floor of his cage. He tested out his legs. Yes—they could do it!

Then, with a great leap that was both forward and upward, he landed at the top of the enclosure.

He hung on, for he thought, "Most surely this is the way out!"

But he was wrong, for too much of his body still hung on the prison side of the enclosure.

For a moment he was puzzled. Then he thrust the claws of his hind legs through the tiny openings of the bamboo cage, got a firm grip, and commenced a frantic effort to push himself up and over the top.

But he had no luck.

Nevertheless, he kept on trying. His forepaws fluttered in the wind. His hind legs beat savagely against the bamboo reeds of his cage. He bellowed. He groaned. He grunted. Foam gushed from his mouth. And pretty soon he went limp. Then, losing his hold, he plunged to the bottom of his cage.

"Oh me!" he moaned. "I'm done for."

Then he forgot everything. And when he came to his senses late that afternoon, there was a very familiar grunt outside his cage. And who should it be but the Little Papa Pig, whom he had met a long time ago down by the riverside.

"Hello there, Mister Crocodile," the Little Papa Pig said, sitting down before the bamboo cage. "What in the world are you doing here, shut up in this cage and miles and miles from the river?"

"I haven't the slightest idea," Mister Crocodile said. "Oh, me. All I know is that yesterday I almost lost my life. I was in a fierce fight. And only the big bite I took in young Beau Gator's neck saved me from being drowned and torn to pieces by the great school of angry alligators determined to get even with me for winning young Miss Gator in The Great Fishbowl Contest."

He closed his eyes a moment, then went on, "But I was fortunate enough to fight my way ashore and to safety and freedom—near the place where I met you some time ago. Remember? You were going to the riverside, and you had a great big load of palmettos to build yourself a little house.

"Well, yesterday it was blazing hot, and like that day when I first met you, I fell asleep. And when I woke up, I was here, all alone in this fearful bamboo cage, miles and miles from my beloved ones and the river. Tell me, Little Papa Pig, how could I have possibly stumbled into such a trap as this in my sleep?"

"You didn't stumble into it," the Little Papa Pig said. "You were brought here by Wiley Wolf."

"Asleep?" Mister Crocodile asked.

"Sure," the Little Papa Pig said.

"But that's impossible!" Mister Crocodile said.

"Nothing is impossible with Wiley Wolf," the Little Papa Pig said. "He found you fast asleep near the riverside, sprinkled you with a bit of the wonderful wild-cherry wine, and then walked you here dream-dead to the whole wide world."

"Oh, me—oh, my! I'm done for!" Mister Crocodile moaned.

"But you're not done for," the Little Papa Pig said. "Once you're tame and trusted, The Forest is a fine place to be. Look at me—I'm treated swell. And look at our old enemy, Bonee Bear. He's been here a long time. Tamed, too. And he's never had it so safe and good in all his born days. Why, he's even been made a patrolman by Wiley Wolf—patrols The Forest day and night. Looks like the real thing, too, with his star and whistle and his big, bluffing bamboo stick."

"But I don't want to stay here!" cried Mister Crocodile. "I want to go back to the river and search for my mate and my beloved little ones."

"Very well, then," the Little Papa Pig said as he went away. "Late tonight, when it's safe, I shall come back and try to help you."

And sure enough, the Little Papa Pig did come back— came back with the escape plans all figured out. And everything started off fine and dandy. He just slid the short end of the long seesaw plank he had brought along over the top of the cage, tipped it downward a bit, then said, "All right. Grab a hold."

Mister Crocodile obeyed.

Then the Little Papa Pig jumped onto the longer end of the plank, bore down with all his might, and old Mister Crocodile flew up into the air with the careless rhythm

of a circus clown. And then, with the greatest of ease, he slid over the top of his bamboo prison and down the seesaw plank to freedom.

"We've made it. We've made it!" he cried aloud.

"We sure have," the Little Papa Pig whispered. "But we're not out of danger yet. Tonight the moon is full, and getting you through The Forest and back to the river is not going to be the easiest job in the world. But we're certainly going to try it."

"Shall we start now?" Mister Crocodile said.

"Yes, in a moment," the Little Pig said.

Then he picked up a gunny sack, gave it one quick shake, and out tumbled a suit of jeans, a soft-brimmed hat, and a red bandana neck piece.

"Oh, I know what these are for," said Mister Crocodile. "They're to make me look like someone else. Right?"

"Right you are!" the Little Papa Pig said. "But come now. Hop into those clothes. Hurry. We've got to keep moving."

Obeying, Mister Crocodile kept on talking.

"You worked this idea once before for me," he said as he slipped into the jeans. "Remember?" He pulled the soft-brimmed hat down to his eyes. "And you got me safely past old Bonee Bear"—he knotted the red bandana at his throat—"and back to the river. A long time ago that was, eh?"

"Right!" the Little Papa Pig said. "But remember— tonight it's a wiser Bonee Bear that we've got to deal with."

They had been walking a long time now, and when they came to the edge of The Forest, the full moon lit up a lone figure trudging toward them.

"Oh, look!" the Little Papa Pig whispered. "Look who's coming—old Bonee Bear, the patrolman of The Forest."

"Oh, what'll I do?" Mister Crocodile cried. "What'll I do now?"

"Act tipsy," the Little Papa Pig advised. "You are dressed in the clothes of the head forester, Wiley Wolf. Once in a while too many sips of the wonderful wild-cherry wine make him tipsy. Then when he takes this road, I go along with him to see that he gets home all right. So now you're Wiley Wolf, the tipsy forestkeeper, and I'm seeing you safely home. Understand?"

"Yes," Mister Crocodile said.

"Here then. Have a nip of this," the Little Papa Pig said. Mister Crocodile obeyed.

"Now put some on your forepaws," the Little Papa Pig ordered. "And rub some on your hat. Some on your coat.

67

And some on your bandana."

Again Mister Crocodile obeyed. And by now the odor of the wonderful wild-cherry wine was everywhere.

"Now we're ready," the Little Papa Pig said.

Bonee Bear was so near now that his silver breast badge and his highly polished bamboo stick, which he swung with such authority, twinkled in the moonlight like stars in the heavens. And he called out with a loud lusty laugh, "Who's that there in the shadows of the trees trying to play a hide-and-seek game with me?"

"It's me," the Little Papa Pig answered. "Me and Wiley Wolf."

"Wiley Wolf," said Bonee Bear. "And tipsy again, eh?"

"No," said the Little Papa Pig. "Not tipsy—just a little tipsy-tickled about catching old Mister Crocodile napping down by the riverside yesterday. So I'm seeing him home."

"Oh, I see," Bonee Bear laughed. "Very well. Go ahead. Keep moving!"

Then Mister Crocodile lunged forward, swayed backward, and, reeling right and left, slumped at the Little Papa Pig's feet. Keeping up his big bluff, the Little Papa Pig cried out, "Oh, come now, Wiley Wolf. Come on. Behave yourself. Do you want Bonee Bear to lock you up with Mister Crocodile?"

Then, as if he were terribly tipsy, too, the Little Papa Pig sang out in a crazy, woozy, wobbly way,

Just a little tipsy-tickled
Tickled tipsy, tickled tipsy!

And foolish old Bonee Bear, doubled up with laughter, called out again, "Very well. Go ahead. You'd better both keep moving while you can!"

9

The Going Home Mix-Up

The news that Mister Crocodile had escaped from his cage raced around The Forest like a shower blown by a hurricane.

"How did he do it?" asked Randy Rabbit, the first to discover the escape.

"I couldn't tell you if my head was off," answered Wiley Wolf.

"A fine thing for the keeper of The Forest to admit," Mister Tortoise teased.

"Someone must have helped him," Perry Possum said. "Otherwise he couldn't have gotten out."

"But who helped him?" Fonee Fox said.

Glancing around the crowd and noticing that Beau Gator was not present, the Little Papa Pig squealed, "Maybe it was Beau Gator!"

"Then run. Make haste and fetch him here," Wiley

Wolf said. And the Little Papa Pig dashed away to execute the command.

"But Mister Crocodile is my mortal enemy!" Beau Gator said when he arrived, panting and out of breath. "Didn't he win the young Miss Gator from me in The Great Fishbowl Contest? And didn't I leave the river in horrible disgrace and come to The Forest to spend the rest of my life in The Big Blue Lake?"

"Well, do you think Mister Crocodile had help in his escape?" Wiley Wolf asked.

"I don't know," Beau Gator said.

"Then let me put it this way," Wiley Wolf said. "Do you think that you, unaided, could leap over the top of this bamboo cage?"

"I don't know," Beau Gator answered.

"Are you willing to try it?" Wiley Wolf asked. "You're about the same size and shape as Mister Crocodile."

"Sure!" Beau Gator said.

"Very well," said Wiley Wolf, "get going."

Inside the cage, Beau Gator made one lazy leap and landed right back in the cage.

Everybody shook with laughter.

"But running here from the far end of The Forest has taken his wind away," the Little Papa Pig said, as he struggled to hold back his chuckles. "Remember—old Mister Crocodile had a whole day to rest up here, and I kinda think he could have managed to jump out by himself."

"Hah!" Fonee Fox grinned. "How come that seesaw plank lying over there is loose?"

All eyes looked toward the seesaw plank.

"Someone go and fetch it here," Wiley Wolf said, snatching a quick glance at the Little Papa Pig.

No one moved.

"Then," said Wiley Wolf, "if no one will go and fetch

the plank here, we'll go and fetch ourselves to the plank!"

Everyone scrambled over to where the seesaw plank lay.

"Notice anything suspicious here?" Fonee Fox asked.

"No, I don't believe I do," Wiley Wolf said.

"But I do," Fonee Fox said. "See those faint traces of footprints outlined on the plank?"

"Yes, I believe I do," Wiley Wolf admitted.

"Well," said Fonee Fox, "they're Mister Crocodile's.

And someone used this plank to help him make his get-away. Yes, I just know that is how he got out."

"Don't make us laugh," the Little Papa Pig said. "Didn't we all—just a moment ago—see Beau Gator come a-panting up here like a tired-out bloodhound?"

"Yes," everyone agreed.

"Well," the Little Papa Pig went on, "I myself saw him race plumb across this seesaw plank. And the footprints that we see here are his."

"But," said Randy Rabbit, "how about turning it over to the other side?"

"It's done," the Little Papa Pig said.

But there were no marks of any kind anywhere on the other side of the seesaw plank.

"How about turning it back to the first side?" Randy Rabbit suggested.

"Sure," the Little Papa Pig agreed. And he dashed to the other end of the plank and flipped it back to its original position. Then Randy Rabbit, leaping upon it, began sniffing a trail from one end to the other.

"Ah-hah!" he hollered. "I smell the smell of a crocodile's smell!"

"Oh, hush your mouth," Wiley Wolf cried. "That's nonsense. All of us know there's a difference in the looks of Mister Crocodile and Beau Gator. But isn't the scent of each the same?"

"I smell the smell of a Little Pig's feet!" Randy Rabbit went on, trying hard to stifle his laugh.

"Sure you do," the Little Papa Pig said. "Didn't I turn the plank over—and from different ends—both times? Sure I did."

And for the first time everyone burst out into the loudest possible laughter.

Randy Rabbit looked very innocent. But he still had his mind set on a good joke and he said, "Say—how come Bubber Baboon isn't here with us today? Maybe he had something to do with Mister Crocodile's escape. And maybe he went along with him."

"Nonsense!" cried Wiley Wolf.

Nevertheless, he turned to Fonee Fox and said, "Run quick and fetch Bubber Baboon here."

"But didn't I run away from the circus to come here?" Bubber Baboon said as he came in for questioning. "And before I came here to live, hadn't I traveled all over the land? And haven't I always said The Forest is the very best home possible for anyone? I know nothing about Mister Crocodile's escape. I slept last night till midnight. Then I went out by the light of the full moon and picked mangoes."

"Good! Good! Very good!" Wiley Wolf said. Then he turned to Bonee Bear. "In your rounds of The Forest last night," he said, "did you notice anything unusual?"

"No," Bonee Bear said. "Nothing. Nothing at all."

"Did you see anyone?" Wiley Wolf asked.

"Yes," said Bonee Bear. "I saw Mister Tortoise with a yellow-bellied catfish in his mouth, Randy Rabbit with a blue-topped turnip, and Bubber Baboon with an armful of mangoes."

"Good! Good! Very good!" said Wiley Wolf. "I guess that's all."

"But that is not all!" Bonee Bear exclaimed. "I saw the Little Papa Pig, too."

"The Little Papa Pig!" Wiley Wolf cried.

"Yes," said Bonee Bear, "the Little Papa Pig! The Little Papa Pig and YOU—walking home by the light of the full moon."

"Good. Good. Very good!" Wiley Wolf said. "Capturing Mister Crocodile made me pretty happy. And I guess I ate too many of the wonderful wild cherries. Anyway, I was a bit tipsy last night. So the Little Papa Pig saw me home."

Everyone shook with laughter.

"But I guess it was just as well," Wiley Wolf went on. "I mean about Mister Crocodile. He's a vicious old thing, and whoever helped his getaway did us all a good turn. But say, Bonee Bear, that must have been two other parties last night that you mistook for the Little Papa Pig and me. We went home early. And there wasn't a speck of moon-light anywhere on the way."

"Fine keeper of The Forest!" Fonee Fox said as they all went away laughing. "He gets so tipsy on the wonderful wild-cherry wine that he thinks the moon's a-shining everywhere. But I hope to tell you, Wiley Wolf, early last night, when you went home, there wasn't a single beam of moonlight anywhere in The Forest."

10

The Long Wait

Mister Tortoise had forgotten all about the escape of Mister Crocodile. And he was all a-quiver with happiness. He was about to become a papa.

When the baby came and it was a son, he was so overcome with joy that he reared up on his hind legs and spun around till he tumbled to the ground, dizzy and exhausted.

"But you're just wasting our time lying there dizzy and exhausted," Mama Tortoise said. "Come now. Get to your feet. Make haste and run to the far end of The Forest and fetch us back a jug of the wonderful wild-cherry wine. It will be good to rub over our son's back. It will keep the bees and beetles and butterflies away. It will make him good and strong. And it will keep the darling little hummingbirds from boring holes into his back. And best of all, it will make him run faster than anyone else in The Forest."

"Right! Right!" Mister Tortoise cried. "More than right you are!"

Then he got up. And rubbing his beak against Mama Tortoise's in a sweet good-by kiss, he set off for the wonderful jug of wild-cherry wine, which he could get only at the far end of The Forest.

But a day, a week—a whole month passed. And there was no return of the beloved Mister Tortoise. Mama Tortoise was sick with worry. But being that way did not bring Mister Tortoise back.

Then one year, two years, five years—ten awful

agonizing years crept by. And Mama Tortoise became lonelier and lonelier, with only the son to keep her company.

But by now even the young son had begun running off to the far parts of The Forest to play and laugh and talk with the other young tortoises of his own age. And they had begun to ask him, "Say—how is it that your father does not return from his faraway journey? We've been told that when you were born he set off to the far end of The Forest for a wonderful jug of the wild-cherry wine to bathe you in. But why doesn't he return? Also, we've heard that your father was present when Bonee Bear was questioned about the escape of Mister Crocodile. Did your father know anything about that escape? Did the full moon that night light up your father coming from the river with a big yellow-bellied catfish in his mouth? And did he see Randy Rabbit flying down the road with a blue-topped turnip? And Bubber Baboon beating down man-goes with a bamboo stick?"

Then, after all these questions, the young tortoises would joke,

Your father this, your father that,
Your father caught a yellow cat.
A yellow cat. A yellow cat.
Your father caught a yellow cat!

More years passed. But the jokes were still made and the questions were still asked about young Mister Tortoise's papa.

Then the young fellow was grown.

"Mama," he said shortly thereafter, "today I'm leaving you. I'm going to a different and faraway part of The Forest. My father does not return, and the cruel jokes of my playmates have made me ashamed. Besides, it's time that I seek a mate. In a different part of The Forest no one will know me—or about my father—and I shall be happy."

Then he was gone.

His Mama was crazy with grief, and only the sudden return of old Mister Tortoise, her long-gone mate, kept her from becoming a regular raving loon.

But she seemed mad indeed when she first greeted old Mister Tortoise.

"What in the world has kept you away for all these years?" she shouted. "You are no good. You've caused me no end of grief. You have caused our son to run away. You have caused—oh, me—you are no good!"

"Me—no good!" Mister Tortoise said. "But look, I've brought back a jug of the wonderful wild-cherry wine!"

"Huh!" Mama Tortoise snapped. "A fine lot of good that'll do us now, with everybody around here talking and joking and laughing about my long wait for your return. And the cruel fate of our only son going off, before he was bathed in the wonderful wild-cherry wine, to a far and different part of The Forest to seek a mate. Yes, a fine lot of good a wonderful jug of the wild-cherry wine will do us *now!*"

"Then away with it," Mister Tortoise said as he sent the jug crashing against a nearby rock. And the wonderful wild-cherry wine, red as the moon at moonset, gushed down over the white rock like the juice of strawberries oozing down over a huge strawberry shortcake. And the scent of it tickled Mama Tortoise's nose like the soft fur of a squirrel's tail.

But she didn't laugh—didn't even smile. She just kept right on weeping and wailing and screaming about the cruel shame and disgrace that Papa Tortoise, by his long absence, had brought down on her and her first-born son.

11

Faster
Than
Thunder

Many days had passed since Mister Tortoise, in a fit of anger for Mama Tortoise's scolding, had sent the wonderful jug of wild-cherry wine crashing against the white rock in their pretty little garden.

Now the thought of his actions brought him great sorrow. And the thought of Mama Tortoise's actions brought her great sorrow, too. She said so. And by and by she smiled about her behavior on that day. And pretty soon she smiled about the whole affair. And by and by she laughed out loud about it. Then one day she said to Mister Tortoise, "Forgive me, darling. Please forgive me for what I said that day, when after my long wait you came back from the far end of The Forest with the wonderful jug of wild-cherry wine and smashed it against the white rock in our pretty little garden. Surely there must have been a reason for your long delay. But no matter what it was—I forgive you!"

"In that case," said Mister Tortoise, with a rainbow of smiles dancing over his face, "I forgive you, too. Now wait here. Wait here and see how quickly I can run to the far end of The Forest and fetch back another jug of the wonderful wild-cherry wine."

Then he was off.

And almost, it seemed, before Mama Tortoise had stopped smiling, the beloved Papa Tortoise was back with another jug of the wonderful wild-cherry wine.

And she, amazed at his speed, said, "But how is it that this time you made the trip so quickly—faster than the sound of thunder?"

"Well, I'll tell you," he said. "It was not the far trip that took so long the first time. It was the wine. This time I just picked the wonderful wild cherries, crushed 'em, drenched myself with a bit of the juice, poured the rest into the jug, and raced back home to you."

Then Papa Tortoise, urged on by the rainbow of smiles still dancing on Mama Tortoise's face, continued with his explanation, "But the first time, after jugging the wine and thinking it needed mellowing, I hung it to age in the fork of a mango tree. Then I crawled into the mud for a nap. The wine made me sleep for a long, long time. And when I woke up, the years had flown. And our first son, grown, lonely, and ashamed of me, had left you all alone and set out to find his first mate in a new and faraway part of The Forest. And all this trouble was the fault of me. But now we have a wonderful new jug of the wine. Hang it from the fork of our own mango tree. And in time it shall be our good fortune to have another son. And we shall bathe him in this wonderful liquid.

"Then," Papa Tortoise finished, "when he's grown and sets off into The Forest, far or near, his proudest boast shall be of that time when his father, faster than the sound of thunder, and with a great big jug of the wonderful wild-cherry wine on his back, raced home from the far end of The Forest and gave him his marvelous, magic birthday bath."

12

The Wonderful Jug of Wild-Cherry Wine

Mister Tortoise's second son was a speed king. Born that way. Leaped from his shell with the zip of a cherry pit shot from a bamboo gun. That's the honest truth. And, bless my soul, if Mama Tortoise didn't have to run and catch and hold him tight for Papa Tortoise to drench him, from head to foot, with the wonderful wild-cherry wine.

But that was just like pouring oil on fire. It only made him run faster and faster. And when he was ten years old, he asked, "Mama, tell me, how come I can outrun all the other young tortoises in The Forest?"

"Because at birth," his Mama told him, "your Papa and me drenched you in the wonderful wild-cherry wine."

"Was my brother, who went to the different and far-away part of The Forest, drenched too?" he asked.

"No, son," Mama Tortoise said.

"Why?" young Mister Tortoise wanted to know.

"Ah, my dear one," Mama Tortoise said, "that is a very sad story, and I would rather not tell it to you now. But when you venture out into the far ends of The Forest, you most certainly will hear it there."

How right Mama Tortoise was! And how well her son remembered her words that day when he was surrounded by a group of young tortoises, and one said, "Although it is clear that you can outrun any one of us here at the far end of The Forest, we are still not too impressed by your swiftness."

"No, we're not," said another, "for it is only the marvelous magic of the wonderful wild-cherry wine that enables a young one like yourself to run so fast."

"Yes," said a third. "We've heard that when your father's first son was born, your mother sent your father to the far end of The Forest for a jug of the wonderful wild-cherry wine. And it was twenty years before your father came back with the wine."

"And your mother scolded your father for his slowness," the first one said.

"And, angered," said the second one, "your father dashed the wonderful jug of wild-cherry wine against a white rock in their pretty little garden."

"And the jug was broken. And the smell of the wine was everywhere," the third young tortoise said. "But none spilled on the back of their long-gone slowpoke of

a son. We are sure of this because we know this son, who is a brother of yours. And we know all his slow-moving young ones, born of the mate he found here at the far end of The Forest. None have been bathed in the wonderful wild-cherry wine, and none can run any faster than we can."

"Hah! Hah!" they all laughed.

"But wait a while," the young Speed King Tortoise said. "If you know my slowpoke of a brother and his slow-moving sons—lead me to where they've hidden through the years. Then you and they shall go home to my father. And you shall all be drenched in the wonderful wild-cherry wine. Then each of you will become, like myself, a speed king."

But the young Speed King Tortoise must have known he was telling a fib. Anyway, when his older and long-gone brother toddled up, bringing with him his sons and all the young tortoises who had heard the boast of the young Speed King Tortoise at the far end of The Forest, old Papa Tortoise said, "A rubdown in the wonderful wild-cherry wine will do you little good now. You've waited too long. I mean, you're all too old. A rubdown can't possibly help you much now. Too late. Too late. Much too late. The very best that you can hope for now is to run and swim a little faster, sleep a little sounder, be a little smarter than the ones who've not had it. That is all. That is all that I can promise."

"But there's still a lot of the wine left from our last son's birth," old Mama Tortoise said. "Here. Rub yourselves down with a bit. Then take some home. Each of you. Hang it from the fork of a mango tree. And when your next sons are born, rub them down gently with it. Rub them down till the marvelous smell of the wine is everywhere."

"Then, when their first borns arrive," old Papa Tortoise ended, with a wide grin on his face, "they shall be able to run, from the far end of The Forest, faster than the sound of thunder, and with a marvelous jug of the wonderful wild-cherry wine."

13

The Little Fisherman

Fonee Fox was wild about fish. He could eat it anytime—morning, noon, or night. And when he wasn't eating it, he was somewhere fishing for it. He fished in The Big Blue Lake, high up in the middle of The Forest. He fished in the river, miles and miles from The Forest, sometimes wading in the water almost up to his chin and ducking and diving and struggling with a great big trout or mullet till he brought it under control. Or sometimes, when the river was black with a great school of mullet rushing upstream from the sea, Fonee Fox would just sit on the shore and wait, quiet as a cat watching a mouse. And it wouldn't be too long before some old gator and his gang would tear into that school of mullet and knock some of them, crazy with fear, into their mouths—or some, squirming and wiggling, high into the air and ashore, where Fonee Fox, with a great upward leap, would catch them in his mouth.

And when he had caught a great big mess this way,

he would build himself a big bamboo basket, put the fish into it, and race back to The Forest. Then, in a little while, everybody for miles around would have his nose tickled with the smell of Fonee Fox's frying fish.

But there were times when he had no luck fishing in either The Big Blue Lake or the river. And it was at such times that he made the rounds of The Forest, sniffing everywhere for a whiff of his favorite food, which, by chance, some of his friends might be preparing. And if the friend happened to be Randy Rabbit, he would strut in and say, "Howdy, Randy Rabbit. Howdy. Now I'll just bet you can't tell where my mind has run."

"No, I don't believe I can," Randy Rabbit would say. "Where's it run?"

"Away yonder on fish. Fried fish!" Fonee Fox would laugh.

Then Randy Rabbit would burst out laughing too. And he'd say, "A thought like that must have come from bathing your head in some of old Mister Tortoise's wonderful wild-cherry wine."

"No. I don't think so," Fonee Fox would say. "It seems to me that right here and now I smell the smell of fresh fried fish!"

But it was no use. He never got anywhere with Randy Rabbit. Nor was he ever clever enough to find out that whenever Randy Rabbit saw him coming, he ran and hid his great big pan of fried fish outside in the fork of a mango tree, leaving nothing inside but the odor of the cooking.

It was a different story, however, with Bonee Bear. Fonee Fox always managed to catch him with an immense pan of fried fish—and out where the whole world could see it. So he would smack his lips and sit down. And as soon as he'd finished, he would jump up and race around The Forest. And everywhere he stopped he would tell about the wonderful fried fish he'd had with Bonee Bear.

"Yes," he'd laugh, "it is really something to talk about. When I sat down, there was a great mountain of fish on the table. But when I got up, there was not even so much as a minnow left. Ha! Ha! Ha! Poor old Bonee Bear!"

Then one day he dropped in on Mister Tortoise. Mama Tortoise was very busy frying a great big mess of plump mullet fish, which the little Speed King Tortoise had just brought back from the river.

"Hello, everybody!" Fonee Fox called out as he strode in. "Is my name in the pot?"

"Well, I sorta expect it is," Mama Tortoise said as she flipped a big, juicy mullet fish over in the pan.

But Papa Tortoise and the little Speed King Tortoise said nothing. No wonder. They were busy thinking of all the stories that had gone flying around The Forest about

Fonee Fox dropping in on Bonee Bear and eating all the fish and then laughing about it behind his back.

But Fonee Fox, still jubilant, said, "Well, if my name's in the pot, Mama Tortoise, I'm too well raised not to come in and sit down."

When dinner was ready, he drew his chair up to one end of the table. Papa Tortoise sat at the other end. At the middle of the long side of the table, and to the right of Papa Tortoise, sat Mama Tortoise. And because it was not proper for young ones to sit at the table with old ones when the old ones had company, the little Speed King Tortoise, who had caught the fish, sat on the floor. But he was facing the table and could watch every move that Fonee Fox made. The great mountain of fish began disappearing like a magician's objects, snatched from the air and hidden in a plug hat. The little Speed King Tortoise coughed noisily. Mama Tortoise shifted uneasily in her set. Papa Tortoise frowned.

When they were down to the last fish, a nice plump mullet, Fonee Fox forked over and got it.

The little Speed King Tortoise tumbled over in a faint. Mama Tortoise dashed to his side. Old Papa Tortoise leaped from his seat, snatched a big bamboo gun from the wall, and, aiming it at Fonee Fox, shouted angrily, "Fonee Fox, doggone your hide—my son hasn't eaten yet, and if you don't put that last fish back on that platter I'm going to blow your blooming head off!"

The fork fell from Fonee Fox's hand as if it were hot with fire. Then he leaped to his feet and ran away without even saying thank you or good-by.

"That will teach the old rascal a lesson," Mama Tortoise said.

"It certainly will," Papa Tortoise agreed.

"And next time he runs around The Forest," said the little Speed King Tortoise, now revived from his faint and nibbling away at the big, browned mullet, "this is one dinner he won't be bragging and boasting and laughing about."

"Right!" said Mama Tortoise as she began fanning her son with a little palm leaf.

14

Full Moon A-Shining

Randy Rabbit strutted into Miss Possum's place as if he'd owned it for a lifetime. No wonder. He was perfectly sure of himself and knew he looked every bit the elegant dandy she thought he was. With his black cutaway coat and his gray striped trousers. With his stiff white shirt. With his Buster Brown collar. With his bright red tie that spread onto his chest like a fan. My, he was simply terrific with his stovepipe hat, tall as a baby and drawn down almost to his left eye. Then there was his gold-headed bamboo cane, flashing through space with the dazzling beauty of a shooting star.

Yes, that night Randy Rabbit looked every bit a dandy. And he was sure Miss Possum would be crazy about going to the Corn Dance with him.

"Howdy!" he said, paying no attention to Perry Possum, Miss Possum's regular beau, also there to take her to the Corn Dance.

"Howdy," Miss Possum said.

"Why, how do you do!" Perry Possum chimed in.

Dropping into his seat without returning the salute, Randy Rabbit crossed his legs, told a few jokes, then got up and said, "Are you ready, honey?"

"Yes, Sugar Pie!" Miss Possum said.

"But where are you going?" Perry Possum cried.

"To the Corn Dance," Miss Possum said.

"But what about me?" Perry Possum protested. "What am I supposed to do? I thought you were going there with me—*alone!*"

"You didn't ask me," Miss Possum said.

"But I took it for granted," Perry Possum said.

"Young fellow," said Randy Rabbit, putting on his stovepipe hat and flashing the gold head of his bamboo cane, "you should never take such serious matters for granted. Besides, long ago, I promised Miss Possum I'd take her to the Corn Dance the next time I called the figures there. I mean like I called 'em that Thanksgiving Night when I had the right turkey drumstick. Now, though, I see you don't want it that way. Jealous, eh? Well, it won't do you any good, because tonight I'm keeping my promise. Come on, honey—let's go!"

And it was then that Perry Possum swooned, plunged forward, and slumped to the floor in a dead faint.

"Oh, I'm dying! I'm dying!" he cried aloud as he came to himself again. "Run quick to Mister Tortoise. Run quick and fetch him back with some medicine!"

Miss Possum, leaving Randy Rabbit behind, ran off.

"Don't worry," Mister Tortoise said when she dashed into his place and told her story. "It's nothing but an old trick that your beau is playing on you. I know. I taught it to him one night—long ago."

"Are you sure?" Miss Possum said.

"Sure I'm sure," Mister Tortoise said. "But I'll take no chances. I'll go right away and see what's wrong. You

must promise me, though, to go on from here alone to the Corn Dance."

"But I can't do that," Miss Possum said. "My company, Randy Rabbit, is still at my place, watching over Perry Possum."

"That's all right," Mister Tortoise said. "As soon as I get there I'll rush your darling Randy Rabbit along to join you at the Corn Dance."

"Very well," Miss Possum said.

Then she was off. And Mister Tortoise, with a bundle of sassafras roots and a bit of the wonderful wild-cherry wine, lit out to treat Perry Possum.

"He's still breathing," Randy Rabbit said, when Mister Tortoise came in.

"Yes, he is," Mister Tortoise agreed. "And I don't doubt that he'll be breathing for a long time to come. You don't know him as I do. This is nothing but a trick he's playing. I know. I taught it to him one night—long ago."

"Honest?" Randy Rabbit said. "And is it the same trick you taught me that time when you rode home on my back from your long-time fishing in the river, and we scared the daylights out of old Fonee Fox in your den?"

"Yes," said Mister Tortoise. "But come now. Put on your stovepipe hat and take your gold-headed cane, and clear out for the Corn Dance. Miss Possum awaits you there. Just another second, though," he added. "What's this? A red carnation, eh? Here, put it in your lapel. I'm sure she meant it for you."

"Thanks for everything," Randy Rabbit said.

Then he was gone.

And a little later, when Perry Possum had been given a nice rubdown with the wonderful wild-cherry wine, he opened his eyes, leaped to his feet, and cried out to Mister Tortoise, "I'm alive! I'm alive! I'm more than alive! And I'm ready for a fling at the big Corn Dance."

Then he, too, was gone.

And at the Corn Dance for a long time, Perry Possum had chatted, called figures, and waltzed Miss Possum around ever so many times before Randy Rabbit, with no wonderful wild-cherry wine rubdown to speed him there, arrived.

"Is there anyone here who came alone?" Randy Rabbit said, as he shot a quick glance around the Corn Dance room.

"Yes, I came alone," Miss Possum said.

"Anyone else?" Randy Rabbit repeated.

"Why—er—I came alone. All by myself," Perry Possum stammered.

"Came *alone*—all by yourself?" said Randy Rabbit.

"Yes," Perry Possum repeated. "Alone."

"Well now," declared Randy Rabbit, "for the girls, coming alone is not so bad. But for the boys, well, for them, I'd say it all depends on the moon. Oh, by the way, Perry Possum, where was the moon when you came in tonight?"

"There was no moon," said Perry Possum. "None at all when I came in."

"Ah," said Randy Rabbit. "That is bad. Very bad indeed. It simply means that you sneaked in. It means that you are scared to be seen alone. It means that you wish to hide from The Queen of the Night the wretched state of your unattached life. And that can only mean . . . "

"But wait a while," Perry Possum cried. "How about you? Didn't you come alone, too?"

"Ah, yes. Indeed I did come alone," Randy Rabbit admitted. "But I came by the light of a full moon. And besides, I thought you were gravely ill, and I came here to take your girl, Miss Possum, home."

The big crowd at the Corn Dance shook with laughter.

"But this is no laughing matter," Randy Rabbit said.

"Perry Possum has committed a grievous error. He has sneaked into the Corn Dance *alone* — and what's worse, in the dark of the night. And because of this frightful folly, he shall not be allowed to call any more figures. Nor shall he be allowed to dance. He shall only be allowed to sit and watch the others as they trip the light fantastic. Is that clear?"

"Yes," everyone agreed.

"Then on with the dance!" Randy Rabbit shouted, as he began singing out the figures.

So that was how it was. Little old Randy Rabbit took over the figure calling at the Corn Dance. And he strode around the room with a heart full of joy.

Then, for a while, he would stop calling figures, grab a hold of little Miss Possum, swing her around a time or two; then to Bonee Bear, sitting high upon a stool and squeezing a big bamboo fiddle tight between his legs, he would holler, "Oh, play that thing, Bonee Bear. Play it till the crack of dawn!"

And away into the night, when the full moon had crept down behind the hills, he went over to Perry Possum, snoozing on a bench in the Corn Dance room. And he shook him right good and hard, and he said, "It's dark outside now, and you'd better get going while there's no one to see you."

"But how about Miss Possum?" Perry Possum said. "Who'll look after her?"

"Ah," laughed Randy Rabbit. "She's dancing into dawn, and she's dancing with me, and she won't go home till the full light of day!"

15

The Dance
of
Bubber Baboon

In a great cloud of dust Wiley Wolf raced up and slid into his place beside the others. They were all there now—Bubber Baboon, Bonee Bear, Beau Gator, old Mister Tortoise, the Little Papa Pig, Randy Rabbit, Fonee Fox, and many others. And they were sitting beside The Big Blue Lake, high up in the middle of The Forest.

"But what kept you so long?" Bonee Bear asked.

"I was waiting for the moonrise," Wiley Wolf said. "You know how important it is to start working on the crops as well as other urgent matters when the moon is just right."

"Yes, that's true," Randy Rabbit said.

They all glanced toward the far end of the lake and saw the moon, just beginning to push its head up from behind the hills.

"There she is!" said Fonee Fox, fixing his eyes first on

the moon and then on Wiley Wolf. "Now what's this urgent matter that you wish to discuss with us tonight? Come now. Speak up. Out with it."

"Then, without beating about the bush," Wiley Wolf said, "I will tell you. I wish to resign as the keeper of The Forest."

"Oh!" everybody said.

"Yes," Wiley Wolf went on, "I've held the honor long enough. So tonight, with a full moon to guide me, I wish to bow out."

"Is it because you lost old Mister Crocodile that time when he leaped from his big bamboo cage, high up in The Forest, and ran back to the river?" asked Fonee Fox.

"No, it's not that," said Wiley Wolf.

"Well, in any case," said Randy Rabbit, "we're awfully sorry to lose you. But who will take your place?"

"That," said Wiley Wolf, "is for you to decide, I mean all of you. See," he said, holding up some corn silk strands, "I've brought these along to guide us in a fair choice."

Then he hid the ends of the corn silk strands in his left paw, and everybody present drew one.

Fonee Fox got the longest strand.

"Does this mean that Fonee Fox is the new keeper of The Forest?" Randy Rabbit asked.

"No," Wiley Wolf said. "It simply means that you, by your votes, will have the chance to select or reject him."

"Oh!" they all said again.

Then the votes were cast. And Fonee Fox got one hundred "yea" votes and two hundred "nay" votes.

"I'm glad he's not our choice," Mister Tortoise said. "Fonee Fox is all right, but he would not make a good keeper of The Forest. He is too crazy about fish. He would spend most of his time fishing—maybe here, in The Big Blue Lake. Or in the river, miles and miles away. Or maybe just strutting around The Forest, sniffing out the places where some mighty good fish was sputtering in the pan."

"That's right," the Little Papa Pig agreed.

So they all drew corn-silk strands again, and this time Beau Gator got the long one. But he was even less popular than Fonee Fox. He polled twenty-five "yea" votes and two hundred and seventy-five "nay" votes. So they all took a final chance, but only after Randy Rabbit had suggested and was authorized to reshuffle and recut the strands.

"But now, how shall we choose our keeper?" Wiley Wolf asked, when two strands, identical in length, had been drawn—one by Bonee Bear, the other by Bubber Baboon —and each had polled one hundred and fifty votes.

"By a contest!" everyone agreed.

"But what kind of *contest?*" Wiley Wolf asked.

"A dancing contest!" Randy Rabbit shouted.

So Bonee Bear leaped to his feet and began his dance. At first it was a slow, easy shuffle. But pretty soon he was whirling around with amazing speed, first with his right foot extended, then with his left foot extended. Then he turned a somersault, landed on his feet, and commenced a fast jig. Then he slowed to a waltz. Then he just stood still and rolled his eyes in a goo-goo way. Shook his shoulders. Quivered his hips. Ballooned his belly in and out. Then he sat down.

The Big Blue Lake echoed with cheers.

Then Bubber Baboon, trembling with excitement, came on. But he began and finished a dance so much like Bonee Bear's that Fonee Fox jumped to his feet and hollered, "Copy cat! Copy cat! Nothing but a copy cat!"

"No! No!" Bubber Baboon cried. "Those are steps I learned a long time ago—before I ran away from the circus. And sometimes on nights like this, when the moon is full and I am lonely for my circus pals, I come here, alone and sad, and do my dancing by The Big Blue Lake. So perhaps Bonee Bear's been spying on me."

"You lie!" Bonee Bear broke out. "You lie a thousand times. Never have I seen anyone do my steps before. I learned 'em all by myself."

"Let's take another vote," Wiley Wolf said, snatching a quick glance at Bonee Bear.

"But I object," said Fonee Fox, "because the way things stand now, it would only come out even again."

"Then let 'em both jump into The Big Blue Lake," Mister Tortoise teased. "And let 'em both do a dance there, with Fonee Fox and his side pulling for Bonee Bear, and Randy Rabbit and his side pulling for Bubber Baboon. That should settle it."

Bubber Baboon laughed.

But all the same, Bonee Bear dived into The Big Blue Lake. In a moment he came up, spitting water in every direction. He swam a few strokes. He snatched quick glances at the crowd on the shore, and diving under again, popped up struggling frantically, with his forepaws aimed at the skies. Another stream of water gushed from his

mouth. His eyes reddened. His ears trembled. His head shook violently. Then, without doing a single dance movement, he swam ashore.

"I'm all in. I'm through," he gasped.

"Then shall I take my turn now?" Bubber Baboon asked.

"No," Wiley Wolf said. "It's quite clear from what we've just seen that no one can dance in The Big Blue Lake. We should have known that Mister Tortoise was only teasing when he suggested that anyone could."

"But I can," said Bubber Baboon, thinking of the smart Randy Rabbit who was pulling so hard for him.

"Perhaps old Beau Gator will leap overboard with Bubber Baboon," Randy Rabbit said. "And perhaps he will swim close to the surface while Bubber Baboon does a water dance on his back. That would really be something, wouldn't it?"

"An excellent idea," Wiley Wolf said. "Let the two try it."

Then Beau Gator and Bubber Baboon plunged into The Big Blue Lake. And Bubber Baboon came up dancing. Dancing just like a man. And he was dancing on old Beau Gator's back! And he danced and danced and danced. And sometimes he called out to those on the shore, "Hey! Look, look! Get a load of this!"

And he'd spin around like a top, tipping old Beau Gator this way and that way, and flinging the rippling waters of The Big Blue Lake in every direction, even away up on the slopes where the watchers sat.

Then he finished.

"But that wasn't fair," Fonee Fox said. "You danced on old Beau Gator's back."

"All the same," Mister Tortoise teased, "it was done in The Big Blue Lake."

"We want Bubber Baboon. We want Bubber Baboon!" Randy Rabbit sang out.

"Very well," Wiley Wolf said. "Your wish is granted."

"Without a vote?" Fonee Fox asked.

"Why, of course," Randy Rabbit said. "Without a single vote. Who'd ever think of taking one now!"

16

Look on Your Back!

After Bubber Baboon had outdanced Bonee Bear that night in the waters of The Big Blue Lake, things got mighty quiet in The Forest. And, for a while, it seemed as if there'd never be any more excitement.

But old Mister Jaybird and Mister Owl, with their fussing and arguing and disputing night and day, changed all that. Indeed they did.

"In the still of the night, when I'm sleepy," said Mister Jaybird, getting Mister Owl told, "you should keep your big mouth shut. You make me tired. You *whoo whoo whoo* all the whole night through."

"In the daytime, when I'm sleepy," Mister Owl argued right back, "you should pipe down on your racket, too. You get on my nerves with your *yap yap yapping* all the whole day long. You should cut it out when I'm sleepy. Do you hear?"

"I'll do nothing of the kind," said Mister Jaybird. "But I'll tell you here and now—if night was made for owls to *whoo whoo whoo* in, then the day was made for jaybirds to *yap yap yap* in!"

So that was how it started. Mister Jaybird kept up his *yap yap yapping* in the daytime, and Mister Owl kept up his *whoo whoo whooing* in the night.

Then, one morning when Mister Owl was taking his daytime nap away down in the hollow of a cypress tree stump near the shores of The Big Blue Lake, Mister Jaybird flew there with a great big bamboo dipper full of water. And he dumped it—*kerwoosh*—right smack into the stump, and the water oozed down onto old Mister Owl's face.

But Mister Owl did not seem to be there. So Mister Jaybird flew back to The Big Blue Lake and got another big bamboo dipper full of water. And he dumped it—*kerwoosh*—right smack into the stump and old Mister Owl's face. But still Mister Owl did not seem to be there. So Mister Jaybird flapped back for a third big bamboo dipper full of water. And he dumped it—*kerwoosh*—into the stump and onto old Mister Owl. And pretty soon a lot of bubbles, about the size of the seeds of the wonderful wild cherries, commenced to ripple up and spread out on the surface of the now-almost-filled hollow of the cypress tree stump. But still there was no sign of old Mister Owl.

So Mister Jaybird flapped back to The Big Blue Lake for the fourth time. And he flew back with another big bamboo dipper full of water. And he dumped it—*kerwoosh*—right into old Mister Owl's sleepy-time stump, filling it smack up to the brim.

And pretty soon, great big bubbles, as big as mango seeds, commenced to whirl up from below, burst on the surface, or tumble, whole, over the brim and float away.

Then all of a sudden—and dripping wet—out popped Mister Owl. He gave himself a wild shake and flung a fine rain of mist into the air. Then he sniffed. Then he snatched quick glances about him.

But he saw nothing of Mister Jaybird. So he just sat there on the edge of the stump, blinking and listening. And pretty soon he heard old Mister Jaybird, away down by The Big Blue Lake, laughing like a crazy loon, "*Yap!*

Yap! Yap!"

So into the air leaped poor old wet Mister Owl. He flapped down to The Big Blue Lake. He tore into Mister Jaybird. He bit him. He pecked him. He clawed him unmercifully. And when he was done, he'd given the old yap-yapper a good and all-round thrashing.

Then he flew back to his stump and just sat there, blinking his red, water-soaked eyes and listening for the *yap yap yap* of Mister Jaybird. But all that he heard was the quiet lapping of the waves on the shores of The Big Blue Lake. So pretty soon, fearful of losing too much sleep for the rest of the day, he crawled into the hollow of a new, dry stump nearby and resumed his nap.

But it seemed that he was scarcely settled in this new resting and hiding place when a big bamboo dipper full of water came tumbling down over him. Again he scrambled from his retreat. Again he shook himself wildly. And he sniffed aloud. And he snatched quick glances about him. And he looked straight ahead, right plumb into the eyes of old Mister Jaybird.

Perched on the first stump that Mister Owl had slept in, Mister Jaybird held in his mouth a big ball of gum, which he had pecked from a sweet gum tree. He lit into Mister Owl. He stuck the big ball of sweet gum onto Mister Owl's back. Then he flew away.

In a flash Mister Owl, with a new wetness and the great big ball of sweet gum still sticking to his back, flew out and after Mister Jaybird. But it was no use. The big ball of sweet gum and his still-wet feathers were too great a handicap for fast flying.

So he could never really overtake old Mister Jaybird. He could only get close enough to him to hear his loud, laughing *yap yap yap* and his big, bold, and mocking command, "Look on your back! Look on your back!"

Then all of a sudden, and before he whirled around to

turn to another dry stump, old Mister Owl gave his head a quick and violent jerk, and there, away up in the middle of the air, he found that his beak was pointed in the opposite direction of his toes. And he could indeed look on his back! And this was marvelous. It was something very special. And it was the first time that he had tried or been able to perform or execute this extraordinary feat.

"Oh, it is wonderful!" he thought as he settled down and slept, undisturbed, in his new, dry stump. "It is very wonderful indeed. And it will come in mighty handy here in The Forest. Handier than a whole night full of *whoo whoo whoo!* Handier than a whole day full of old Mister Jaybird's loud and loony *yap yap yap!*"

17

The Run
of the
Forest

The Little Papa Pig was in serious trouble. No wonder.
The news had leaked out that he had helped Mister
Crocodile escape from the big bamboo cage high up in
The Forest. Everybody was furious with him for such a
rash act, and so almost every move Little Papa Pig made
for help was turned down.

"I'm sorry," said Bubber Baboon. "You were all for
me that night when I danced in The Big Blue Lake, and
I'd like very much to help you now. But I don't dare do
it. Bonee Bear and Wiley Wolf would skin me alive."

"Then, if you can't help," the Little Papa Pig said,
"how about some suggestions? Come now. Look. What
would you advise me to do?"

"Ah," Bubber Baboon beamed. "Advice? That's possible. And pretty easy too. But you must promise to keep
your big mouth shut. Do you hear?"

"I solemnly promise," the Little Papa Pig said.

"Then run quickly around The Forest," Bubber Baboon said. "Tell everybody that you've been to see me. Say that I'm very angry. Say that I'll listen to no plan for forgiveness that does not include your running down to the river and fetching back Mister Crocodile, with his promise to stay in The Forest for the rest of his days. Say that you . . ."

"Hold it," the Little Papa Pig said. "That's enough to guide me. Look—I'm on my way!"

Then he was gone.

"Poor Little Papa Pig!" Bubber Baboon thought as his little friend disappeared in a great cloud of dust. "He will never be forgiven because he will never be able to fetch back Mister Crocodile. How foolish of him to try!"

But even at that very moment the Little Papa Pig was making some plans to prove that Bubber Baboon could be wrong. His swift journey around The Forest included a long stay and chat with his old friend, Mister Tortoise.

"Fetching Mister Crocodile back to The Forest is not impossible," said Mister Tortoise, as he gave the Little Papa Pig a good rubdown with the wonderful wild-cherry wine. "But it won't be easy. During the day, keep a close watch by the river. And if you get hungry of a night, run back here and I'll have food and drink and another rubdown in the wonderful wild-cherry wine for you. Is that clear?"

"Yes," the Little Papa Pig said.

"All right then, be off," Mister Tortoise urged. "And just in case you might need it for something before you return, here is a bit of the wonderful wild-cherry wine to take along with you."

For days and days the Little Papa Pig haunted the banks of the river at the edge of The Forest. But no Mister Crocodile came ashore.

Then one night, when he returned to the riverside after a bite to eat and another long chat with his friend Mister Tortoise, there he was—Mister Crocodile—lying on the shore!

"Hello there!" the Little Papa Pig called.

"Oh, hello," Mister Crocodile called back.

"I've been looking for you for a long time," the Little Papa Pig said. "I'm in trouble again."

"I'm in trouble, too," Mister Crocodile confessed.

Then the two old friends exchanged reports of their predicaments.

"I think I can help you," the Little Papa Pig said. "And

116

I think you might help me too. Isn't what you most long for your mate, the young Miss Gator, and her young ones?"

"Yes," said Mister Crocodile, coming closer to the Little Papa Pig.

"And if you could swim faster than anyone else in the river," the Little Papa Pig went on, "wouldn't you be able to make a better search for your long-lost loved ones —carried away by the new Beau Gator and his gang?"

"Sure I would," Mister Crocodile said.

"Then here's the help," the Little Papa Pig said. And he gave his friend a good rubdown in the wonderful wild-cherry wine and sent him on his way.

His return was faster than the sound of thunder.

"Ask any favor of me you wish," he said to the Little Papa Pig as he scrambled ashore with his mate and his wonderful brood of long-lost loved ones. "Ask any favor of me at all, and I shall grant it."

"Then," the Little Papa Pig pleaded, "grant me the favor that was first asked of you: come back to The Forest with me."

"Good!" Mister Crocodile grunted. "Your wish is granted."

Then, turning to his long-lost Miss Gator and their wonderful brood of young ones, he said, "We're going now, with the Little Papa Pig, to an enchanting place called The Forest. There we'll find food and sunshine—and a big blue lake to swim in. And everyone there—even the big Beau Gator who once made so much trouble for us in the river—is friendly!"

Then, when the Little Papa Pig had rubbed everyone down with a bit of the wonderful wild-cherry wine, they all raced, together, to The Forest.

"I don't believe they'll be with us long—unless they're caged!" Wiley Wolf said that morning when everyone in

The Forest had been called out for an opinion.

"I quite agree with you," Bonee Bear said.

"But we should give them a fair chance to see if things work out," the Little Papa Pig said.

"Yes, that's right," Bubber Baboon agreed.

"Caging them will do no good," Mister Tortoise volunteered, "because they've all been rubbed in the wonderful wild-cherry wine, and they can leap as high as the sky."

"Well, not so high as the sky," Mister Crocodile laughed. "But all of us can leap quite a little."

Then, to prove his point, he jumped into and out of the nearby bamboo cage with the greatest of ease, his body forming a circle in such a way as to make him look like a big hoop with bamboo spokes rolling down the hill.

Then, one by one, Miss Gator and the big brood of young ones, leaping in and out of the cage, duplicated Mister Crocodile's amazing feat.

"Looks like something I did in the circus a long time ago," Bubber Baboon said.

Everyone applauded.

The Little Papa Pig was warmly praised. Then Wiley Wolf and Bonee Bear, ashamed of themselves for what they had said earlier, shuffled away.

"The run of The Forest is yours," Bubber Baboon said. "We hope you like it. You'll find friends here. And food too—plenty. Bananas. Oranges. Mangoes. Fish in The Big Blue Lake. Berries for making the wonderful wild-cherry wine. Everything!"

"We sure do thank you," Mister Crocodile said, glancing a smile in the direction of the Little Papa Pig.

"Don't mention it," the Little Papa Pig grinned, "the pleasure's all ours. And I'll bet you'll be as happy here as old Mister Jaybird, full of the juice of the wonderful wild-cherry wine."

18

The Big Bamboo Boat Race

"Well, the boats are all ready now," Bonee Bear said as they met that glorious summer afternoon, under a palm tree high up in the middle of The Forest, near The Big Blue Lake. "Shall we go down to the lakeside to inspect them?"

"Yes, indeed," old Beau Gator said. "I'm just dying to see what kind of racing boats you've been able to fashion out of bamboo reeds."

"Me, too," Mister Crocodile said, fixing his eyes on old Beau Gator. "After all, the race this afternoon is between you and me, isn't it?"

"Sure," old Beau Gator said.

"Come on then," Randy Rabbit said. "Cut out the gabbing and let's get going."

Then they were at the lakeside. And they saw the two beautiful bamboo boats, which were really more like barges, bobbing up and down on the water.

"Now," said Bonee Bear, with a twinkle in his eyes and a nod to old Beau Gator, "perhaps you will tell us why The Big Bamboo Boat Race is going to be staged today between you and Mister Crocodile."

"Certainly," old Beau Gator said. "I'll be glad to. It's being staged, I'm happy to say, to give me a chance to make an honorable return to my kinsmen in the river, miles and miles from here."

"But I thought you were happy here," Fonee Fox said, "high up in the middle of The Forest, in this beautiful blue lake where there's so much of everything to enjoy."

"Happy?" old Beau Gator said. "Yes, in a way. But who can be completely happy without his honor and a mate?"

Then, turning to Mister Crocodile who'd soon be his rival in The Big Bamboo Boat Race, he said, "Tell them. Tell them, please, Mister Crocodile, how I lost my honor and the chance of a mate in The Great Fishbowl Contest last year at the full of the moon."

"Sure. Sure I'll tell them," Mister Crocodile said. "Listen. Old Beau Gator lost his honor and his chance to choose a mate by just one tiny little fish in The Great Fishbowl Contest at the full of the moon last year. That is to say, I was able, with a terrific whack of my tail, to land just one more fish then he into the shell-ringed circle in The Great Fishbowl. And that made me the winner. And it sent me strutting from The Great Fishbowl with the young Miss Gator here, by my side, as a mate."

"Oh!" they all said.

"Yes, that's right," old Beau Gator said. "Mister Crocodile is telling the truth. And after that, all I could hear down in the river and in The Great Fishbowl was a silly little song that always poked fun at me and said,

Beau Gator this, Beau Gator that,
Beau Gator slapped a flying bat,
But when he had a fish to twirl
Beau Gator went and lost his girl!

"So," Mister Crocodile said, "you ran away from the river and The Great Fishbowl and made your way to The Big Blue Lake, high up in the middle of The Forest, eh?"

"Yes," old Beau Gator said.

"Well," said Mister Crocodile, "in your race against me today, I might as well tell you, I'm going to win."

Then Wiley Wolf stepped forward and said, "Now that most matters are all settled and we're just about ready for the race, who'll tell us how it's going to be conducted?

And who's going to lay down the rules that will govern the contest? And why has there been so much secrecy in these matters?"

Bonee Bear leaped to his feet.

"There has been no secrecy about the rules," he said. "I've simply been quiet about them because I wished to give each of the contestants an equal chance. So here, now, are the rules: each boat—or barge, as I'd like to call it—will have on board a creature of the same size. He will be at the rudder to guide the barge. There shall be no one else on board. Randy Rabbit will be at the rudder on Mister Crocodile's barge. Fonee Fox will act in a similar capacity on old Beau Gator's barge."

"But what about Mister Crocodile and Beau Gator?" Randy Rabbit asked. "Who's going to row the barges?"

"Keep your big mouth shut!" Fonee Fox said.

Everybody laughed.

"There'll be no rowing," Bonee Bear said. "If I had wanted rowers, I would have built row boats for the race instead of barges. But I didn't want rowers. I wanted swimmers. Good swimmers. See those long bamboo poles that run across the far ends of the barges? They almost touch the water, don't they?"

Everybody nodded.

"Well," Bonee Bear continued, "when Mister Crocodile and old Beau Gator are in the water and all set to go, those bamboo poles are for them to catch hold of with their big strong mouths. Then they will commence to squirm and twist and paddle with their forepaws and hind paws and their big long tails till they're at top speed and moving right along toward the finishing rope that old Bubber Baboon has stretched good and tight across the far end of the lake—away down yonder. Look, look. Can you see it? It's stretched all tight in the sunlight and just waiting for the first touch of the winner."

123

Again they all nodded.

"But suppose they both touch the finishing rope at the same time?" Randy Rabbit wanted to know.

"That can hardly happen," Bubber Baboon said.

"Suppose, though, it just did happen," Randy Rabbit said.

"Well," said Bubber Baboon, "I don't think there's one chance in a hundred for a draw because as soon as they're off we're all going to trot along the shore of the lake to watch their progress. And if they're even when they're pretty close to the homestretch, Wiley Wolf will blow his bamboo whistle, and that will be a signal for the racers to cut loose from their barges, dive beneath them, come up on the forward end, then strike out for the finishing rope, completely free of the barges."

"But even then," Randy Rabbit said, "they could reach the finishing rope at the same time."

"Well, in that case," Bubber Baboon said, "the race will be won by the swimmer who grabs hold of the rope and gnaws his way across the line and to victory. But someone is going to have a pretty hard time doing that because I myself made that rope, and it's good and tough and strong and made of Spanish moss rolled into a thin long line and stuck together with sweet-gum sap, drawn from trees high up in The Forest."

And so, with the rules of the race all clear, old Beau Gator and Mister Crocodile plunged into the water of The Big Blue Lake and pushed their barges steadily ahead in the direction of victory. And sometimes it was Beau Gator who was in the lead, and sometimes it was Mister Crocodile.

But when they had covered more than two thirds of the distance and neither was ahead of the other, Bonee Bear said to Wiley Wolf, "I think you'd better blow your whistle now."

"Yes, I was just going to," Wiley Wolf said as he shrieked out a warning to the contestants, now nearing the end of the race and swimming with all their might.

Down into the water and under the barges they plunged, sending a great collection of bubbles swirling to the surface and shining all golden in the sunlight.

Then they came up. Came up near the bow end of the barges, blew great mouthfuls of water into the air, and struck out for the finishing rope.

Now they were even. Now Mister Crocodile was about half an inch ahead. Now Beau Gator was ahead. Once again it was Mister Crocodile who led. Now they were even again. Each swam with all his might, churning up the water in a great white and swirling foam. Both let out loud and desperate bellows. Both hit the finishing rope at the same time. Each chewed with all his might. But it was old Beau Gator, with his bigger, stronger and double-shovel-like mouth, who first bit the rope in two and sent poor Mister Crocodile, still gnawing with all his might, zig-zagging off in the water toward his deserted barge.

Everyone cheered.

Then old Beau Gator scrambled ashore. He leaped to his feet, spun around on the tip of his tail, then let out a long line of whoops and hollers that echoed around The Big Blue Lake like a great roll of thunder. Then he sang sort of soft and low,

The Big Bamboo Boat Race!
OUooo! — OUooo! — OUooo!
Over the water, under the water,
And through the water too —
The Big Bamboo Boat Race —
OUooo! — OUooo! — OUooo!

And every creature around The Big Blue Lake knew that old Beau Gator had won The Big Bamboo Boat Race.

And they all came rushing to his side.

But he still spun around on the tip of his tail. And he still sang. And now his forelegs and hind legs flapped in the wind like the sleeves and legs of a scarecrow. Pretty soon, though, he dropped to the ground—*kerplop*—and when he'd caught his breath, he said,

"I'm sure glad I won. It puts behind me the shame of losing to Mister Crocodile last summer in The Great Fishbowl Contest. And now, with my head held high in pride, I'm going back to the river to win myself a loving mate. And I'll bring her back with me. And we'll live forever and ever right here in the wonderful joys of The Big Blue Lake."

Then he was gone. Gone to win himself a mate in The Great Fishbowl Contest down by the riverside.